The

Unicorn

Moms

The Unicorn Moms

Book 1

In

The Unicorn Series

By

Mary O'Hora

Acknowledgements

A unicorn is a mythical and magical creature. Deep down, we know they don't actually exist, but we can't help secretly wishing they did.

In 2018, I was fortunate enough to meet a rare group of women who I also thought were mythical creatures. Women who supported each other; who laughed together and held each other up.

A small group who enjoys each other's company despite our different cultures and beliefs. We respect our differences and celebrate our similarities.

Although this series is completely fictional, it is ultimately inspired by these fabulicious girls.

So, without further ado,

Renee, Stephanie, Mouna and Shelby,

this one is for you, biches!

Charlotte

1ˢᵗ Tuesday

"Levi…. Levi? Can you hear me?"

"Yes, jeesh, calm down, what's the problem?" My 15-year-old son barely looks at me as he slopes into the kitchen.

"I thought you said, you cleaned up in here?" I swipe the crumbs from the counter, onto the floor with my hand.

"Oh, yeah, I forgot…" he picks up a kitchen cloth without rinsing it and starts wiping down the granite breakfast bar.

"You haven't even emptied the dishwasher!" Steam escapes as I fling open the door. I count to ten in my head, knowing this isn't worth losing my cool over. I look over at Levi, his dirty blond hair drapes across his left eye, dishevelled yet handsome without even trying. My lazy, unmotivated teenager.

"Mom, I'm sorry, I got distracted. I'll get these chores done now." He gives me a half-smile, which immediately dissipates my anger. He's just a kid, a good kid. If not doing his chores is as bad as he gets, then I'll count my blessings.

"I'm going for a shower; we're leaving here in 30 minutes. It's your first rehearsal, we can't be late." I'm not even sure if Levi is listening as he pops his headphones back on his ears. I enter my room to grab my towel and clothes.

"Grace, honey, did you tidy up in here?" Our bed is neatly made, Folded laundry sits on the edge, waiting to be put in the drawers.

"I just thought I'd tidy up so it would be nice for you." She smiles at me as she puts Adam's socks and boxers into his top drawer.

If ever a child was aptly named, it was Grace. Content and full of goodness. I would love to take credit for her, but she was born with this beautiful disposition.

"You are the best ever. Do you know that?" I wrap my arms around her and feel her squeeze back tight. "Are you ready to go shortly?" The question is redundant really, Grace is always ready, but I knew she was nervous about joining this new theatre group.

"Yep, I'm good. Don't forget we're picking up Karla and Adriana on the way."

"I'm on it," I call back as I leave the room. I had totally forgotten. So, in actual fact, I now have only twenty minutes to shower and change. I turn up the volume on my phone and select my *shower jams* playlist. Five minutes of belting out my favourite Celine songs and I'm washed and dressed. With only fifteen minutes left, it's hair or makeup, no time to do both. I apply a little tinted moisturizer, a quick stroke of blush and a thin coat of mascara. I gather my hair into a high pony and tease it into a messy bun. I assess my overall appearance in the mirror. A forty-five-year-old woman stares back at me. The dark circles under my eyes are not quite concealed by my light makeup. My long flowing blouse can't hide the fact that I'm fifty pounds overweight, but I leave the top few buttons open, to distract the eye from my waist. My smile is wide and reaches all the way to my eyes. I look good enough.

I sit at my vanity and attempt a short 5-minute meditation to calm my anxiety. I hate meeting new people. I feel awkward and over talk. I worry about seeming too forward or confident, so then talk more, all the while wishing I could shut myself up. When the kids were smaller, it was easier. I talked and played with them at their different clubs. Now they were teenagers, they would run off and find new friends in minutes at every activity and I would be left looking around at the other moms, reluctant and awkward.

They no longer need me to hold their hand, but they still need a taxi. A few last-minute deep breaths and I head downstairs to search for my shoes in the hallway closet.

"Levi, Grace, c'mon please, let's go." I holler so they might hear me in their rooms.

"Coming," I hear Levi call back as Grace joins me at the door. As we walk to the car, the cold wind whips around my face and I hurry to my bright red Jeep. I crank on the heat and turn up the radio. Grace slides into the passenger seat with a cheeky smile, happy to have grabbed the seat before Levi.

The door to the back seat opens and Levi slides in, smelling of aftershave and toothpaste.

"Why'd we have to leave so early anyway?" he catches my eye in the rear-view mirror.

"We need to pick up Karla and Adriana." Grace turned from her front seat to explain to him.

"Gabrielle is teaching at the studio, and I said we could give the girls a ride. It will save her from having to rush around." Karla and Adriana are the same ages as Levi and Grace.

I had become unlikely friends with Gabrielle over the years, through playdates and church bake sales. She's fiery and

4

determined. We're probably too similar in some manners, like magnets, we can repel each other. She's more like a sister to me now. We love each other and annoy each other equally. My Irish passion occasionally conflicts with her Brazilian flair, but so far there have been no casualties.

I pull the car into their driveway and honk the Jeep's horn to let the girls know I'm here. They make their way to the car and join Levi on the back bench.

"Hey guys, how's it going." I sing-song at them as I manoeuvre the Jeep in reverse.

"I'm good," smiles Karla. "Me too," joins Adriana.

"Awesome, everyone excited for rehearsal?" I look around the car while stopped at the traffic lights and 4 uncertain faces hesitantly smile back at me.

"I feel a bit nervous; I hope we'll know some people."

"Me too, Karla, but a least we'll all know each other." Laughs Grace, always the optimist.

The girls chatter excitedly while Levi concentrates on his game. I'm sure he's nervous too. Not easy being the new boy at 15, but I am proud of him for joining this theatre group and I hope he will make some new friends.

I pull into a space in the large parking lot, and we make our way towards the church. I realize we are a bit early as we enter the almost vacant hall.

"Hi there, I'm Michelle." A voice calls out from behind the piano in the corner. The woman stands to greet us. It seems as though she glides towards us, her flowing skirt, hiding the movements of her feet.

"Hi, we're the Owens and the Bach's. I'm Charlotte and these are my children, Levi and Grace. I've also brought Karla and Adriana with me today." Michelle smiles at all the kids.

"It's great to meet you all. I'm wondering if you wouldn't mind helping me put the chairs out, before all the others arrive." She asks the kids, who are milling in front of her.

"Sure, where would you like them laid out." I feel proud of Levi who is quick to offer assistance. Michelle outlines where she needs the chairs placed and all 4 kids set to work. There are some tables off to the left and a stack of chairs, which I presume are for any parents. I grab a chair from the stack and place myself at the corner of a table, trying to look inconspicuous in the vast, empty room. Michelle returns to her piano, and I watch as the kids lay out over seventy chairs in their semi-circle rows.

More children arrive with their parents and the hall quickly fills up. I busy myself in the corner, with my phone, avoiding catching anyone's eye. Hoping to just fade into the background.

"Welcome Everyone." Michelle stands in front of the now filled chairs with her arms outstretched. "I'm excited to see so many of you here today and I'm just going to lay out a few ground rules."

I tune out and sort through my emails. These 2-hour rehearsals are going to be twice a week for the next 8 weeks, and I fully intend to use this time productively. Reading, online shopping, and updating my Pinterest board. Things I no longer find time for running a busy household.

"Ello, do you mind if I join you?" I look up to see who owns this breathless French accent and nod at the dark-haired woman beside me. She pulls up a chair with her perfectly manicured hands and I instantly fold mine into my lap, embarrassed at the chipped purple polish I hastily applied last week.

"I'm Monique." She flashes me a bright white smile framed by her full red lips. Her cheekbones look taut on her perfectly made-up face.

"Hey, I'm Charlotte, nice to meet you," I smile back at her. "Are you new to this group also?" She looks like she fits in wherever she goes. I can feel my heart pumping rapidly as my breath quickens. I try few deep breaths as subtle as I can. I can't imagine Monique feeling new or awkward anywhere.

"Oh no, my little Olivier has been singing and dancing since he was five. This will be his third year in this group. I have no talents; I cannot imagine where he gets it from." Her French accent drips off each word as though she had just flown in from Paris. She shrugs out of her black tailored coat and smooths down her perfectly coiffed, gleaming hair.

"So, Charlotte, is this your child's first time joining the group?"

"Yes, I have Levi, in the back row there, wearing the white hoodie, and Grace in the third row is also mine." I point out my kids to her.

"This is wonderful, your Levi looks around the same age as my Olivier, he is also 15, no?" She looks at me expectantly.

"Umhmm, yes." I have no idea what she has just said, I am distracted by the music of her accent and those friggen amazing cheekbones.

"Well Charlotte, I am so 'appy Olivier will have a new friend, maybe me too." She winks at me jokingly. I burst out laughing. I had been nervous and hiding away, and here was the enchanting Monique willing to be friends. Maybe this theatre group won't be so bad after all. I mean, nothing can be worse than those dance Moms from last year.

"Quiet please, that includes parents. Thank you." Michelle's voice booms through the hall and I notice a few of the other parents looking over at Monique and me.

"Oops, we're on the naughty list now," I whisper over to Monique as she lifts her chair to sit closer to me, just inches away.

I can now breathe in the heady scent of jasmine and a kind of deep, warm musk. She even smells sophisticated. She probably wears a perfume you can only buy at the boutique. I glance sideways to get a better look at her now she's so close, and to my dismay, she looks just as perfect up close.

"Don't worry about Michelle, she likes to be very stern at the first rehearsal to show the new kiddies what's what, but it isn't always tense like this. You will see, Charlotte, we have a wonderful little theatre family. You will love it, no?" She doesn't just look awesome; she is genuine and sincere. She is exactly the kind of woman you want to hate, but I can tell it would be futile to even try. I'm sure everyone eventually falls under Monique's spell. Her charm is absolutely hypnotising.

"No, I mean yes, yes, I'm sure I'll love it, thank you, Monique. I was nervous. I didn't love hanging out at Grace's dance rehearsals last season." Oh, why did I just admit all that to this perfectly pulled together woman? Here I was over talking, as usual. *Shut up, Char.*

"Oh, dance moms are the worst! No, we are not like that here, well some maybe." She laughs as she nods her head towards a blond lady who was taking notes of everything Michelle was informing the kids on. I hadn't brought any paper or pen.

"Am I supposed to be taking notes?" I bend down to grab my bag. Maybe I have something to scribble with inside it.

9

"No Charlotte, that is just Linda, she needs to make sure she misses nothing. She and her daughter Reese, like everything to perfection. She's a much better Mom than us, no point even competing." I look surprisingly at Monique and as the corner of her eyes crease, I can see there is more to this beauty than I first thought.

"Ha ha, you got me good Monique." I feel my shoulders drop as I relax a little more. I sense I am going to get on with her. She isn't quite as innocent and nice as she first appeared; just my kind of friend. Genuine and kind, but peel back a few layers and a sassy bitch lay underneath.

"Mom, you've got to come and sign a copy of the group's rules. Michelle said no one can leave without completing it." Grace is at my side, her face flush with excitement, keen to make a good impression.

"Okay Grace, I'm coming, say hello to Monique."

"Hi Monique, I'm Grace." My beautiful girl smiles up at my new friend and I see she finds her as enchanting as I do.

"Grace, I'm so happy to meet you and your maman also, I will see you girlies on Thursday, no?" I am getting used to her finishing her sentences with a questioning no. If it were anyone else, it would be annoying, but Monique sounds sultry and playful without even trying.

"Sure, we'll see you then," I push in my chair and follow Grace towards Michelle who is handing out the group rules.

"Here you are, Mrs. Owens. Levi and Grace did really well today, they're going to be great additions to the group." Michelle passes me the form, and I grab a pen from the table to sign its receipt.

"Oh, please call me Charlotte." I return the pen and look around for Levi. I wave over to him to signal we were ready to go.

"Great, thanks Charlotte, I hope the kids enjoyed their first session." She looks at Grace, who was beaming from ear to ear.

"I love it and I'm gonna go home and download all the music so I can practice even more." Safe to say, all of Grace's worry and anxiousness are long forgotten. I smile over at Michelle, thankful my daughter has loved the experience.

"Hey, Mom, I'm ready." Levi joins us as we say goodbye to Michelle, and we make our way outside to the Jeep.

"Char! Thank you so much for bringing the girls, it is so nice of you to help me out." Gabrielle is parked beside us and is calling out to me from inside her warm vehicle. I can see the steam where the hot air from her vehicle is meeting the bitter cold.

"My pleasure beautiful, It's no sweat! See you Thursday." I call as I yank the car door open. It's too cold out and I'm not freezing my ass off for anyone. I wave as they pull out.

"Guys, we gotta get a remote start for this car. It's too cold for my old bones." Luckily, the heat was quick to warm, but I hated the cold which a Canadian winter could bring.

"I know Grace loved it, but what about you, Levi?" I look at him sitting beside me. He had nabbed the passenger seat this time.

"Yeah, it seemed alright. There were a couple of other boys that seemed cool, I think it'll be good." This was a rave review by Levi's standards, and I give myself a mental pat on the back. I knew this theatre group would be awesome for the kids and maybe it would be good for me too.

Monique

1st Thursday

"Oh, I just love it. I don't think my face has felt this good in years. Thank you, Monique. You truly are a miracle worker." Mrs. Dawson runs the back of her hand across her cheek, smiling at the smoothness.

"You're so welcome, Mrs. Dawson, I am so glad you like this cucumber face peel. It's part of a new range I'm trying out." I'll be able to use this experience as further proof to Irene that we need to expand the salon's treatments to stay competitive. I've been working here at Village Spa since the year after Juliette was born. 10 years is a long time. I love my job and my clients, but now Olivier and Juliette are older, I am hoping for more hours at work. If we don't expand our treatments and entice new customers to the spa, I don't know what will happen. My client list has dwindled over the years, as other salons have kept up with the latest trends and products, but Irene, who's owned the salon for thirty-five years, has refused to progress with the times.

"Well, you have a great weekend ahead Monique and I'll be sure to let the ladies in my bridge group know about this wonderful peel." Mrs. Dawson interrupts my reverie as she waves goodbye from the salon door. With only 10 minutes until closing, I print off the day's receipts and balance the float in the till. Only 3 customers all day, I'm not sure how Irene is even covering the rent with so little profits. I sweep the entranceway, sanitize the surfaces, and write Irene a note about the new face peels. I check the appointment book for tomorrow to discover she only has two clients booked in for the day. A salon with only two clients on a Friday is a worrying sign.

A last-minute glance around the foyer to check nothing is out of place, and I grab my jacket from the closet. I fashion my soft purple cashmere scarf into a rolled loop in the mirror and fuss with it, until it falls in place, looking effortless. I love scarves, well any accessories really, fashion in general. It's my passion. In my twenties I had dreamed of being a fashion designer in Haute Couture, but being swept off my feet by Marc and quickly pregnant with Olivier had soon put a hold on those girlish dreams.

I give the salon door a firm pull to assure myself it is locked and head across the street to my car. My boots already damp in the dirty melting slush. I run through my mental list of jobs I need to tackle this evening on my drive home. Trying to remember if I took the chicken out of the freezer for dinner or if I need to ask Marc to grab something.

As I turn onto our street, I can see Marc's red truck already in the drive. He was home early. Maybe he'll have started on dinner and saved me a chore. A girl can dream, can't she?

"Allo, mon Amour." I smile at this handsome man as he meets me in the foyer. He helps me out of my jacket and grabs a hanger to hang it in the closet.

"Did you have a perfect day, Chérie?" he unwraps the scarf tenderly from my neck as he leans in to kiss me softly. He smells of cologne; a rich, heady scent that suits his dark brooding looks. He teasingly bites my top lip and I smile at his playfulness.

"Maman, come and see what I've got." Juliette bounds down the stairs and grabs my arm, tugging me to follow her into the kitchen. Reluctantly, Marc loosens his grip and gives me a determined look that says 'we will finish this off later'.

"Wow, Juliette, where did you get all this from? It's fantastique!" On the table before me, she has laid out her collection of dolls. Her favourite one, Chelsea, is dressed in a sumptuous fur coat with a matching hat. I pick up the doll and inspect her coat. A

15

red satin lining and even little pockets. Some stray threads need tidying, but overall, the craftsmanship is excellent.

"I'm so glad you love it. It's taken me weeks to complete. I think I've unpicked more stitches than I've sewn. It's the hardest thing I've made so far, but once I trim the edges with ribbon, I think it will be perfect." I beam at my beautiful 11-year-old daughter. She has loved dressing up since she was just a little girl, and I have never missed an occasion to share my love of fashion with her. Now, here she was, creating her own styles. They were for her dolls, admittedly, but the details are there. I can tell she has a great eye. Taking the simplest fabrics and introducing the perfect trim to turn it into a statement piece. My heart is overflowing with pride.

"I can't believe you made this yourself, Juju. I wish I had one this pretty. Chelsea will be warm all winter." I tease her fondly with a smile.

"One day, Maman, when I'm working in Paris or Madrid, I'll make you this same coat and then you'll also be warm all winter." She wraps her arms around me and I squeeze her back.

"Juliette, your Maman already has me to keep her warm, don't you worry." Marc informs our daughter as he joins in our hug, wrapping us both up in a bear grip. Juliette starts giggling as Marc softly tickles her.

"Marc, why are you home so early?" I disentangle myself from them and open the fridge. The empty glass shelf stares back at me accusingly. I had forgotten to take the chicken out. I open the pantry to see what I can throw together.

"It was a crazy day at the salon. I had eight customers booked in for the day and then that imbecile Gareth tried to add two more on this afternoon. You know, Monique, I realized the salon has three stylists, but I see over half the clients. Gareth could have taken those extra two bookings himself, or even asked Dina, but no, he put them on me. Well, I thought enough is enough, and I walked up to Gareth and I told him, 'Au revoir mon ami.' Marc dramatically throws his arm into the air as if performing some kind of magic trick.

"Marc, you left your job? You just walked out?" I could hear the worry and panic in my voice.

"Chérie, don't worry, Gareth will be begging me by this evening to come back and I'll negotiate a pay raise, while I'm at it." I should have known Marc has a plan. He always does.

"Well, I only had 3 clients today and takings are down at the spa, I'm worried Irene will be cut my hours even more soon. The last thing we need is for both of us to be out of work." I can feel the frown lines form on my forehead and I massage them away with my hands. I have enough on my plate. I don't need to add wrinkles to the list.

17

"Monique, you are too good for Irene's little parlor anyway. This is the sign you have needed, time to find something new." Easy for Marc to say. He was always so confident and optimistic. I had worked hard over the years, and the idea of having to start all over again felt like failure.

"I know you mean well, but I'm older now and it would be hard to start over." It's difficult to admit to Marc that I'm scared.

"What is this old you speak of? You, Monique, could never be old. You are as beautiful as the day I met you. No, I am wrong, you are more *magnifique* now than even back then!" His hands caress my face as he stares into my eyes. "*Chérie*, you are perfection, and don't you forget it. Any salon will snap you up if old Irene doesn't appreciate you. Don't worry yourself with such trivialities." I smile back at him as I lean into his reassuring embrace. Marc could make you feel invincible. His belief in the people he loves is contagious. I know he still sees me as that 23-year-old girl he met along the Seine all those years ago, and I am grateful he keeps the image alive. Reminding me of who I am, when I falter.

"We've got to be at rehearsal in 40 minutes and I haven't even made us supper." I hate for the kids to not have a home-cooked meal in the evenings.

"Tell the kids to grab a snack and pick us up a Chinese on your way home from theatre group. I'll light a fire and we can have a picnic on the rug in the front room." There are some real advantages to having married a hopeless French romantic. I smile at him in agreement and go to change out of my work outfit.

"Olivier, be ready in twenty minutes, please," I call out as I run up the stairs. Once in my room, I undress and throw my work clothes in the hamper. I pull on my leggings with a cowl neck sweater. Warm and cozy is what I need for the cold, damp church hall.

"Maman, tea is ready." I can hear Juliette beckon me from downstairs. I lightly dust my face with some bronzer and grab a lip gloss to take with me.

"Juju, you made me tea? Thank you so much, just what I need before rehearsals." I love how she has set the cup in a saucer and added a side plate with 2 of the ginger wood mill cookies that are my weakness. She knows I will only eat one and leave the second for her. It's our little unspoken game.

I feel the stress and worries from the day disappear. I am off on Fridays, so I have the entire weekend to relax and unwind.

"I'm going to work on my school project, Maman, or I would come this evening to keep you company." Juliette is my mini me, my best friend, and she doesn't like me to be alone. She is the caretaker of our family. Always watching out for each one of us.

"Actually, I think the lady I was telling you about from last week will be great company for me." I had already recounted to my family, how my new friend and I were scolded for our laughter. I do like to be at the centre of any mischievousness and the new mom, Charlotte, seems like she will be good fun once she loosens up a bit.

"That's great, I won't have to worry you're on your own. I'm going to set up my work in my room, I'll tell Olivier it's time to go. Love you." She finishes as she bends down and kisses my cheek. I squeeze her arm and smile at her. So full of care and love for others.

I popped my head into the garage to find Marc before I leave. I knew I'd find him here. He is sprawled out on the old couch at the far end, by the door. He smiles at me lazily as he blows smoke from his nose.

"Ahhh Monique, a little relaxer before rehearsal?" His outstretched hand offers me the joint he is holding between his thumb and forefinger.

"Maybe when I get back, don't wanna be told off for more giggling at rehearsals." I reprimand him. We laugh. It's easy with Marc, we laugh a lot.

"Maman?" I hear Olivier looking for me. With a quick kiss, I leave Marc to his languishing and head to the front door.

"How was your day?" I haven't seen Olivier yet today and I'm eager to catch up on our way out to the car.

"The usual, nothing much." I sense this is the end of the conversation as he closes the car door and turns up the radio. 15-year-old boys don't like to chat and gossip with their moms. I sing along to the radio and we make it across town in just minutes. I pull into one of the last available spots in the parking lot and we make our way towards the hall.

It's busy tonight. I should have arrived a bit earlier. Now I will be stuck standing awkwardly by the back wall or forced to sit next to Linda or Sandra, an even worse fate. Olivier joins the rest of his age group, and I contemplate going back out and sitting in my warm car when I see a flash in the far corner of the room. It's Charlotte. She is waving her arm and the glass of her watch is reflecting the light and signalling to me like a beacon on a lighthouse.

I smile and make my way towards her, determined to avoid both Linda and Sandra who I can sense are pushing their chairs towards me. Not today, thank you ladies. Not ever.

"Charlotte, you've saved me a spot, thank you so much." She was removing her coat and bag from the chair, clearly left there to reserve my place.

"I wasn't sure if you came to every rehearsal and I could see that red-haired lady giving me evils over there." She tilts her head towards Sandra and I wasn't surprised. Sandra is one of the most annoying moms in this group, actually the most annoying in our town, maybe the world. She and her even more whiny, annoying teenager, Drew.

"Ignore Sandra, she seems intimidating, but she's only a Mom'ager. She thinks her kid will be the one who makes it, and she revolves her life around managing all her schedules and activities. Don't ever get caught asking her about anything. She'll bore you to death with her ten-year plan." Charlotte peers over at Sandra and I can see she is seeing her in a different light, as she looks back at me and smiles. She is cute, this new woman. I got the impression on Tuesday she was of a nervous disposition, but I suspect she will be a lot of fun once I break down her barriers.

"I brought you a coffee, I hope it's not weird. I just didn't want to have one for myself only. I'm sorry, I'm babbling again." I smile, her social awkwardness is endearing.

"This is so thoughtful of you, thanks." I pick up the steaming cup and take a sip.

"There's sugar and cream in the bag and I also have a little something to keep the cold out if you're interested?" I realize Charlotte is a complete minx as she passes me a small tiffany style flask filled with brandy.

"Cheers." She clinks her cardboard cup against mine."

"Chin Chin," I reply, and we both dissolve into giggling schoolgirls, despite the weary look from the other parents.

Stephanie

1st Thursday

I can feel my blood boil as it courses through my veins, gaining momentum. Something has gone wrong. I'm awake in the middle of a nightmare.

I open Nate's drawers and start throwing his clothes on the bed. It doesn't help. I feel even angrier. "Stephanie, I know you're upset, but there's no need to behave so childishly." Nate looks at me with disdain, as he calmly continues to pack his things into the large suitcase, open on the bed.

"Childish? I'm childish? Wow, Nate, you really have no shame. You've been caught with your pants down and you have the audacity to call me childish? Well, I haven't even started, let me tell you!" I didn't think I could get any madder, yet here I was, now enraged. I pick up the glass bottle of cologne on top of the drawers and bring it close to my nose. Hoping its sandalwood undertones will bring calmness and remind me of the good times we have shared together. Nothing. I cannot remember one single good time. Our entire past is now tainted with his infidelity. Without thinking, I hurl the bottle at his head. I watch in shock at my own actions as Nate bends down to reach for a fallen shirt. The bottle narrowly misses his head and thumps into the wall behind him.

"Stephanie! What in the hell is wrong with you? I could have been seriously hurt." Nate looks at me in shock.

"You know who's actually hurt right now, Nate? Me. That's who! I wish you hadn't ducked. I wish the bottle had hit you and you could have a scar for life to remind you of the disgusting, lying, cheating, despicable man you are! How dare you play the victim." I can see the spittle flying in the air as I spit my words out at him. I feel unhinged.

"You know what Steph, the truth hurts. If you had been a more attentive wife, maybe I wouldn't have needed to look elsewhere. You could have made more of an effort to keep yourself in shape." I look around for something else to lob at him. In an instant, I understand how a completely sane person could be driven to harm another human being. I wish he were dead. The pain and cruelty he is inflicting on me is making me deranged and I am honestly scared of what I might do next.

"Mommy, is everything ok?" A scared little voice breaks my trance. My angelic Lucy is standing in the doorway. Her eyes dart back and forth nervously between Nate and me, tears sliding down her cheeks. My anger leaves immediately as I register the pain on her frightened face. I rush over to her and kneel down to wipe away the tears.

"I'm sorry, Lucy. Mommy and daddy are having a disagreement. I didn't mean to scare you." I hug her but she pulls back and looks at me questioningly.

"Why is Daddy packing his suitcase? Is he going somewhere? Are we all going somewhere?" I can see her last thought is hopeful like maybe we are all going on holiday. I long for that to be true.

"No, just daddy, sweetheart. He's gonna go to Grandma's for a little bit, so there's no more fighting." I would do anything to rewind the clock and save my child from the realization that our family is falling apart. Nate continues to pack his bag as though we are a freak sideshow, he has nothing to do with.

Lucy walks towards the bed. "Don't you love us anymore, Daddy? Is that why you're never home? Is that why you need to leave?" As I hear her words echo in the vast room, I feel ashamed.

I had allowed Nate's disinterest in me, in us as a family, and now it was affecting my kid's self esteem.

"Of course, I love you, Lucy. You'll always be my number one girl. Right now, I just need some space away from Mommy." Great, put the blame on me, you fucking douchebag.

"C'mon Lucy, why don't I make us some hot chocolate." I hold my hand out to her. As she slips her cool, small hand in mine, I vow not to let Nate's despicable actions hurt my children any further. I am their Mom; I will protect them.

I distract myself by preparing the hot chocolates and try to resist the urge to run back upstairs for round two with Nate. I know it's futile. It will only upset me and the kids further. I don't think Nate can hear me, anyway. He seems to be solely focused on his own needs right now. I wonder if he's having a midlife crisis? Maybe a bit of a breakdown? Couldn't he have just bought a Corvette like Jim down the street?

"Mom, are you making hot chocolate for me too?" I didn't notice Liam enter the room and join Lucy at the breakfast bar. His cheeks look flush and as I study him closer; I can see he's been crying. My sweet, tough boy. Fuck you, Nate! Fuck you for hurting me and hurting our kids. You selfish prick!

It takes every ounce of self-control I have left not to grab a knife from the block and run back up those stairs to put an end to all the misery I know lays ahead of us.

"Sure, I am, Liam, I've even got extra marshmallows." I give him a lopsided smile. He knows I am hurt and I know he is sad, but we are both trying to shelter Lucy from it. Even my 12-year-old son has more decency than the man I have shared my bed with for the last fourteen years.

"Mom, are we still going to the theatre tonight?" Lucy's small voice reminds me, life goes on in a crisis, the world keeps turning. There's no way I can drag myself there this evening.

"Oh Lucy, I don't think I'm up for it to be honest. Maybe we can skip just this one?" I know she won't go for this, it only started earlier this week.

"Mom, you signed the rules, we can only miss 2 practices out of the entire schedule." Liam joins in. "Maybe dad can take us?" he offers. I know he doesn't want to miss the rehearsal, but he doesn't want to force me to go if I don't feel up to it, either.

"I will go and speak to your dad and see what we can organize." Reluctantly, I make my way upstairs dreading having to approach Nate for help. I enter our bedroom as he is zipping up a second suitcase.

"The kids want to know if you can take them to rehearsals?" I don't look at him as he moves his cases closer to the doorway.

"What time does it end? I have plans later."

"You have plans? On the day you are leaving your wife and kids, you already have plans? What kind of scumbag are you?" I am incredulous. Seemingly, my husband has more important plans than leaving me and his kids.

"There's no need for all this name-calling, Steph."

Nate is using his reasonable voice, trying to be an adult and have the upper hand on me.

"Well, Nathaniel dick-for-brains, I very much disagree. I think there is every God damn need for some fucking name-calling, ok?" I yell into his face. Merely inches between us.

"You don't hear me accusing you. You don't hear me blaming you and your flappy bird for having to look elsewhere, do you Steph? No, you don't, so grow up!" The hate and disdain in his words shoot through me, each one like a bullet coming out clean the other side.

"My flappy bird? Is that a saying? Is that even a thing? Just when I thought I couldn't hate you anymore, Nate, once again, you've proved me wrong." How had I ever married such a vile man? How many years have I remained blind to his atrocious behaviour? I should never have let things get this bad. Why didn't I walk out years ago when I still had a shred of self-respect left? I am done pleading and negotiating with this man. I am done being his victim.

"You can drop the kids off on your way out of here and I'll pick them up when it's over. Leave your key on the hall table, Nate. There will never, ever be any coming back from this." He looks at me almost sadly and nods. I make my way to leave but pause in the doorway. "Nate?" I wait for him to look over at me and he turns towards me wearily. "Take a mental picture of this house and this life we've built, so in the months to come, when you wonder where it all went wrong, you can rewind to this moment. You can remember it was all your fault." I know my words aren't registering with him, but I feel better having said them.

I return to the kitchen and let the kids know their dad will drop them off and I'll pick them up when rehearsal is finished. I remind them to grab their song binders, and take my hot chocolate into the playroom. I sit on the big armchair in the corner, remembering the years I have sat in this room, watching the kids grow and learn. I am frightened to think what lay ahead of us now. Will we have to move? Will I need to get a job? I have no back-up plan. I was so busy building this life and trying to make it work, that I hadn't planned for when it would all go wrong.

"We're leaving now, Mom. Will you be, ok?" I hear the concern in Liam's voice. I look up at him in the doorway, left half ajar.

"I'll be fine, sweetheart. I'll be there to pick you up, ok?" I smile to reassure him but as he nods solemnly, I know I'm not fooling him.

I hear the heavy front door shut, and I contemplate the surrounding silence. This is it, Steph. This is what you get. 14 years and not even a commemorative pin or a toaster as a thank you. If I had put that same amount of time and effort into a job, at least they would have offered me a redundancy package. Yet, here I am, without even so much as a thanks. I sit in a daze for over an hour. Too many thoughts whirling in my head to stop on just one.

Eventually, I get up and make my way to the master bathroom. I wash my face and try to put some order into my hair. I can't tame it, so I hastily wrap a bandana around the whole mess. I will wait in my car until the last minute to grab the kids and avoid seeing anyone.

As I walk out the front door, I see Nate's key on the entranceway table, defiantly reminding me of the day's events. I slam the door behind me and concentrate on making my way to the church in one piece.

Once I arrive at the church, I park in one of the few spots left available, close to the door.

I fiddle with the radio knob. The current station is belting out Pop songs, and I am finding it increasingly annoying. I settle on a station with has a man's soothing voice.

"Wherever you are, whatever you're dealing with, you are not alone." The deep voice seems to caress me in my car.

"We are all in this thing called life together." I lay my head back on the seat and let this hypnotic voice relax me.

"We are all God's children." Oh my God, I am tuned into the Christian music radio station! I'm not exactly an atheist, but on my best days I am skeptical about any higher power and today was certainly not the day to start believing. As the opening notes of Hallelujah fill the car, I am frozen. The words rouse every emotion in my being as tears course down my face. The music wrenches every fibre in my body as the grief spills out of me. My top has damp spots on it from the never-ending flow of tears. I start wailing with the music, cathartic, letting all my feelings and hurt release with each and every resounding word.

I hear a knock and I realize I am still in my car, outside the church. I had forgotten where I was. I look up and see two women staring at me in concern. I want to die. Just when I thought this day couldn't possibly get worse, I had outdone myself! Wailing to

Christian music and having a mental breakdown in my car in front of two other Moms.

If I ignore them, maybe they'll leave. I glance to the side and see the brown-haired mumsy woman, looking straight at me with grave concern. I can tell she is going nowhere.

"I'm ok." I gesture with a wave of my hand as I roll down the window.

"Honey, I'm sorry to disturb you, but you don't look ok and we were wondering if we could get in with you, it's cold out here? We only nipped out for a cigarette and then heard you and, um, your music." I sense this woman liked to take charge of things. Organized and controlled. I don't want to be taken charge of. I want to be left alone.

"It's no problem, we don't mean to disturb you. We just wanted to check you were ok." Now the black-haired lady is speaking to me with her heavy French accent. I can hear the kindness in her tone and it sets off a new bout of crying.

"I'm sorry," I call out to them as I press the unlock button for the doors. Both women slip into the backseat of my car. I sit crying for another minute or two until the French one passes me a handkerchief.

"It's ok *Chérie*, we are here if you need us." She reassures me as I wipe a trail of snot from my face with the beautiful linen fabric, she has lent me.

"I'm sorry you've had to see me like this. I'm not normally this much of a mess. Well, actually, I am always a hot mess but not normally in this sad, self-pity kind of way." I try to explain to these kind strangers.

"Honey, we're all hot messes. That's what it is to be a Mom. We're just the same Monique and I, aren't we Monique?"

"Ah, even on my best days, I am a mess underneath." Confesses Monique. I turn in my seat and take in this beautiful woman who looks like she has just walked out of a catalogue.

"Well Monique, excuse me if I don't believe you." I eye her up and down. I know I am being rude, but this perfectly put-together woman has no idea how I feel right now and I doubt she ever could.

"No need to hold back, honey, you just let it all out." The matter of fact one is clearly unfazed by my attitude. I realize I'm not going to get rid of these women that easily.

"Thanks, ladies, I appreciate your concern, but I think I would be best left on my own right now." I give them a half-hearted smile in an attempt to thank them, but also to reassure them. I'm hoping they will now leave.

"Of course, we understand completely, don't we, Charlotte?" Monique's tone is soothing and kind, I am regretting my earlier dismissal of her.

"Yes, for sure, but honey, if you don't want us to wait with you, should I at least go in and fetch your child to save you from the bright lights in there?" I was right, Charlotte is a fixer. Already organising and planning how I can extract my kids and get out of here. I had hastily judged these women. They were only trying to help.

"Oh, yes. I hadn't thought about actually going in and collecting Lucy and Liam. I was hoping they would just come out."

"Oh, no Mme Michelle, won't let the kiddies come out on their own. Charlotte is right. Let her go in and get them a minute or two early and then you can slink off and no one will see you, yes?" I nod in agreement. I can see these women are determined to help me, it's easier to give in.

"Rehearsal ends in 5 minutes, so I'll go get your kiddos ready and Monique will sit here with you, ok?"

"Sure. Thanks Monique and Charlotte. I appreciate what you're trying to do for me. By the way, I'm Steph." They both smile at me and Charlotte makes her way back into the building.

"Well Stephanie, I am glad I was out having a smoke just at the right moment. I am going to step out of the car and have another one now. I don't want to alarm your kiddies with some strange woman in the car, that's ok, no?" She steps out of the car and closes the door softly, reappearing by my window. I roll it down and feel some of my anxiety and sadness escape out into the cool night air.

"Thanks Monique, you and Charlotte have been very kind, I don't mean to act so ungratefully. I've just really had an awful day." I try to explain my actions but fall flat.

"Not at all, Stephanie. I cannot imagine what would put a woman into such a state, but if I had to guess, I would think only a man could render any woman as beautiful as you into such a sad mess. All men are pigs!" A sad mess? Monique clearly has a way with words!

"Thanks, Monique." I manage as I see the kids running towards my car, with Charlotte behind them.

"Hey Mom, why didn't you come......." Liam's voice trails off as he looks at my ravaged, tear-stained face.

"It was time to go anyway." Lucy tells him, always ready to rush to my defence.

Charlotte reaches into the car and rubs my shoulder. "Steph, it's been great to meet you, and no hiding away in your car next week. Come down and join Monique and me. I'll save you a seat with us and I'll bring you a coffee." I can see it would be pointless to refuse this kind but bossy woman.

"Thanks Charlotte, you and Monique have been lovely." I smile at my two intruders as I push the button to close the window. With a small wave, they make their way back into the hall.

"Mom, who were those women?" Lucy is inquisitive.

"Oh, they just came over to talk to me and check I was ok in my car on my own." I certainly don't want to admit to my kids that I had been wailing in my car.

"Oh, that was kind." Lucy smiles at me.

"I thought we were in trouble when the bossy one came to get us." Liam pipes up.

"Oh, that's Charlotte, I think that's just her way. She's clearly a force to be reckoned with." It was silly, I felt the need to defend these women.

"See mom, it's not just us who make new friends at our groups, you have too now." Lucy smiles at me, delighted to find yet another silver lining.

I put the car in drive, and we make our way home. I can't imagine how I will confess to my family and old friends that they had all been right. Nate is a complete dick. Unless I wanted to eat a lot of humble pie, I was gonna need some new friends.

Charlotte

2nd Tuesday

"Allo Charlotte, I guess this is our usual table now." Monique poses her bag on the table, as she unwraps her scarf and slips out of her coat. "It's very warm in here today, I don't think I need all these layers," she smiles as she takes the seat opposite me.

I wonder what kind of job Monique has that she always looks so elegant. "Did you come straight from work?" I wonder.

She shakes her head as she reaches for the coffee I've left in the middle of the table. "No, Fridays are my days off, so I run around town and get all my chores done."

"So, this is your casual, Mom about town look?" I tease, and she pretends to swat at me.

"You, Charlotte, are a minx! I like to look nice, even if it is my day off, but I have days when I sit around in my Pyjamas with spilt cereal down my top, just like everyone else." She raises her eyebrow and taps the top of her cup.

"Oh, is this a secret signal?" I mock her as I reach for the flask in my bag and slide it across the table.

"Hi Charlotte, hi Monique," Steph smiles at us awkwardly as she reaches our table.

"Allo Stephanie, how are you, *Chérie*?" Monique pats Steph on the arm.

"I'm good, thanks. Well, maybe not good, but better than you both saw me last week."

Her hair looks freshly styled, complimenting her natural make up. She looks about 10 years younger than the first time I saw her, last Thursday, "you look good, I really like your hair like that."

"You know what they say, are you even going through a breakup if you don't change your hair?" she's laughing it off, but I can see the pain cast a shadow across her face.

"Oh Stephanie, good for you. You are clearly a powerful woman and better off without him." Monique passes her a coffee with the flask and Steph looks back at us disbelievingly.

She laughs and tips a generous shot into her drink, "I thought you girls were joking about the brandy so I wouldn't feel like such a mess the other night." She takes a large gulp and closes her eyes as the brandy warms her throat.

"I know you don't believe me, but I'm a total hot mess too. You're not alone," I reassure her. I can tell by the way she's studying me that she's reassessing her first impression.

Monique leans forward to share a secret with us, "yes, me too," she confides. I highly doubt it and I look over at Steph and catch her rolling her eyes. The two of us burst out laughing as Monique sits back in her chair, crossing her arms in a fake pout.

"Well, not only have you insulted me, but I can see Linda, Sandra, oh and even Catherine looking over here none too happy with your noise." She smirks at us.

I push my coffee to the side and lean forward, "what is with those women? Are they Michelle's assistants or something? That Sandra one gives me a once over every time I see her. Like what is her problem?" I look towards the miserable redhead on the other side of the room, shaking my head.

"Oh, Sandra thinks her little Drew is going to be an overnight wonder. I wish her child would become a success so I wouldn't have to see her anymore. She is everywhere I go. Swim lessons, soccer, and now has even moved to the same school as my Juliette." I'm relieved I'm not the only one who gets bad vibes from her.

"Well, I'll be staying out of her way," Steph declares. "Who are the other two then?" she encourages Monique.

"Linda is the blonde one knitting, she's Reese's mom." She points out a blond girl with pigtails in the front row, singing a little too eagerly. "Reese won the county music festival last year, and her Mom is determined to tell everyone she meets. She volunteers for anything and everything that can help her daughter get a foot in the door." It dawns on me; these moms might be even worse than last year's dance moms.

Monique pours another shot of brandy into her coffee and takes a sip before continuing. "Then we have Catherine, she's the one with the sleek bob." we glance over at the dark-haired businesswoman. She has discreetly set up a laptop at a table in the back of the room. Oblivious to our stares, she is jotting things down on a notepad from her screen. Her manner is intense. "Her daughter is Lexi, the one in the Michael Kors boots." I know straight away which kid Monique is describing. The girl would not look out of place on a runway. For such a small child, she commanded presence.

"I'm not sure if this is the right place for Lucy or Liam. It all sounds a bit intense, but they need the distraction if I'm honest," Steph sighs.

"Well, luckily for you Monique, Steph and I are here now to save you from the drama moms." I wink at them.

"Yes, it's fantastique! We can be the hot mess moms together," Monique darts a glance at each of us and we laugh quietly, aware the other parents are sending 'looks' our way.

The ping of a text message interrupts us, and Steph fishes her phone from her pocket. A frown overtakes her smile as she reads the message. She hastily shoves the phone back into her coat. "You ok, Steph?" It's obvious the message has upset her.

"It's my husband, or I guess soon to be ex-husband, Nate." she explains, "he wanted to let me know that he's found a place to rent and needs to talk to me about money. He's not sure he can afford our mortgage and his new place."

"Have you been separated long, Stephanie?" Monique asks softly.

"He only left last Thursday when you met me in the parking lot. He was going to stay at his moms for a while, but I'm guessing that's not working for him and his new girlfriend."

"That's awful, I'm sorry Steph. He sounds like a real piece of work." I feel sad for my new friend. I've only just met her, but I know without a doubt that she deserves better than this loser.

Monique nods in agreement and takes Steph's hand in hers, "you must get a lawyer, Stephanie. Don't enter any agreements until you've talked to someone. My friend Isabelle, she got ripped off by hcr husband because he drew up a 'fair' plan and the poor thing signed it, only to find out later she was entitled to a lot more than he was giving her." She clasps her hand tightly, urging her to take her advice.

A silent tear escapes down Steph's cheek, "I haven't worked in years. I've just stayed home with the kids. I don't know what I'm gonna do." She wipes another tear with her sleeve as Monique and I reassure her, she has options. "It's just so hard. I'm trying to be strong for the kids, but I'm lost. I can't get any support as it would be wrapped in 'I told you so's' and 'we tried to warn you's'. I don't have anyone to talk to." She looks into her lap, embarrassed to have told us the ugly truth.

I was quick to dispel her fears, "you do have people, you have us," I pick up my phone and pass it to her, "enter your number so I can text you mine, you too Monique. I'll make a three-way chat for us all. We can promise there will be nothing but support and laughter in our group. How does that sound?" Steph lifts her head and smiles. This time I can see it's a genuine smile.

"Mom, come meet my new friend," Grace runs up to the table excitedly and we all stand to gather our things. "Reese, over here, come meet my mom," Grace waves at the eager young girl and I hear Stephanie snort across the table. I look over as she and Monique are making faces at each other and nodding in my direction. Yep, trust my loving and caring Grace to make friends with the daughter of the mom who already dislikes me for no reason!

"Hi Reese, nice to meet you," I smile at her.

"Hi, Grace's mom, do you think Grace could come over and hang out one day?" she asks. I inform the girls we have a long season ahead and there will be plenty of time for get-togethers. "Come and meet my mom Grace," Reese grabs her arm and drags her off.

Steph grabs Monique's arm and mimics the girls playfully, "wanna come and meet my mom, Monique?" the two of them are delighted with themselves. "Charlotte, maybe you should go over and arrange a playdate with Linda." Mocks Steph. She and Monique almost fall over, bent with laughter like two schoolgirls, drunk at their first disco.

"No more brandies for you two," I scold them, "you're both on the naughty list now." I give them my stern look to let them know the joke is over.

"Ohhh, watch out Stephanie, that sounds like an official warning," we can barely understand Monique, her accent now mixed with tears of laughter.

"I'm going to find my kids, before I lose the only friends I have," Steph is still laughing. It's clear neither woman is taking my attitude seriously. I take out my phone and type out a text in a new group message.

Both of their phone's ping, and I watch as they both read the message. **Please accept this as a written warning you are**

currently on the naughty list. They catch each other's eye and continue their ridiculous hilarity. The few remaining parents are definitely giving us looks.

I feel my phone vibrate and reluctantly take it out of my bag as they watch expectantly. **Charlotte, please accept my apology. Also, when you go for coffee with your new friend Linda, can I come too? Steph x** I roll my eyes and stare her down. She stares back at me intently and in spite of myself, I join in their silly mirth.

$\wp \infty \wp$

As the kiddos and I enter the house, I hear Adam singing in the kitchen. The music is loud, so he doesn't hear us. We watch as he stirs the pot with a wooden spoon and lifts it as a microphone crooning over the stove. He does a half twirl and stops dead as he faces us, realizing he has an audience.

"Way to go, dad," Grace applauds him. His cheeks look flush, maybe from the cooking but more likely from being caught in his one-man kitchen concert.

I kiss his cheek, "watcha cooking, good looking?" I tease him. He puts the wooden spoon back into the pot and brings it to my lips, "mmmm… chili."

Adam is a fantastic cook. The spices tingle on my tongue. "How was rehearsal guys? Levi, Grace?" he puts down the spoon and turns down the stove top, offering them his full attention.

"Yeah, it was good. Hey dad, didn't you used to play guitar? Do you think you could teach me?" I was surprised at Levi's request. Normally you couldn't force him into anything that didn't involve gaming.

"Well, I'm a little rusty now, but I'm sure I can teach you the basics." Adam demonstrates his skills with a little air guitar. Levi and Grace join in and I laugh at them. "Come on Char, loosen up, show us your moves," he goads me. He knows I don't like to embarrass myself; I'm not joining in. He dances his way over to me and takes my hand. Twirling me like a ballerina. He rolls me back to him and nuzzles my neck with his stubble, reducing me to a giggling mess with his tickling.

"Enough, Adam, or I'll pee my pants and then I'll be mad for real." I chide him. Grace and Levi are egging him on. "Ok, you two, grab a snack and get ready for bed," I order in the most mom voice I can muster.

"Shall I also get ready for bed?" Adam reaches to tickle me and I quickly step out of his reach. He's persistent, I'll give him that. My lovable, fun, easy-going husband.

I know people look at him and wonder how he ended up with me, but since the day I met Adam, he has always been the one. People think I'm high strung and controlling, but Adam doesn't see me like that. I worry about problems that don't exist. I expect the worst-case scenario so I constantly prepare for all eventualities. It's exhausting, but I don't know how to be any other way. Luckily, Adam does. He has always known what buttons to push and when to push them. When to soothe, when to calm, even when to tease. He teaches me how to find the fun in life. He allows me to figure out who I am and who I want to be.

As I look at him with a twinkle in his eye, I feel desire soar through me. "Yes Adam, I think it's way past your bedtime actually." And I run towards our bedroom with no doubt that he is right behind me.

Monique

2nd Thursday

How can the salon be such a mess when we've only had two clients so far today? I pick up the nail polish bottles on the manicure table and put them back on the display shelves. Irene comes through the front door with coffees and her lunch.

"Monique, I grabbed you a coffee, to keep you going," Irene passes me the cup and I smile my thanks. She sits at the recently cleaned manicure station and unwraps her lunch. I can smell it from here, egg salad sandwiches. I turn away as I feel the urge to retch. There is a small kitchen at the back of the salon, why doesn't she simply eat back there? I pull my cowl scarf closer to my face and inhale my perfume in an attempt to calm my churning stomach.

I move to the opposite side of the room and begin taking inventory of the new face peels. We've used 7 so far. I bring up the supplier's website and look to see what other new offerings we could add in.

I'm engrossed in an introductory video on a new product called jelly feet. You sink your feet into a jelly mix and when it sets you remove your feet, peeling back the jelly layers to reveal smoother feet. Apparently, it's all the rage amongst the younger generations. It looks gimmicky, but it holds a high profit margin, so I add a ten-piece sampler pack into the cart. I didn't hear Irene approach behind me, but the smell instantly makes me aware of her looking over my shoulder. "These jelly feet look worth a try, Irene. I see the face peels are already doing well. I'm excited with this new supplier's line, they have a lot of innovative and fun products to encourage a younger customer base." I move aside to let her see the screen more clearly and to distance myself from her eggy breath.

"Monique, I have been running this spa for over 30 years and have stayed with most of the same suppliers since my beginning days. Fads and trends have come and gone, but me and my little salon are still here." She proudly informs me. Poor Irene, she couldn't accept that her little spa was hanging on by the skin of its teeth. It was her lack of vision and willingness to jump onto these trends that had lost her so many clients over the years. There were a few other spas in our town, and even though none of them had the experience or expertise that Irene or I had, they offered a much wider range of products. They stayed on top of the latest trends, leaving us at the Village Spa behind.

"It would help if we could entice some younger clients as well though, don't you think Irene? It's great to have our regulars, but look at the bookings sheet, we have no one in for the rest of the day. The older generation plans ahead and makes appointments. We need to target some of the younger, more whimsical clientele to help us fill up our quiet times, no? Have you thought more on my suggestion to open some social media accounts for the spa, to connect with potential new clients through there?" I may as well open the whole can of worms now that I had started.

Irene picks up one of the face peel treatments and reads the ingredients. "These peels don't have half of the benefits that my old oatmeal scrubs offer, and they're twice the price, I just can't see why anyone would be interested," she put the sachet back and looked at me expectantly.

"Sadly, I don't think people are really looking at the ingredients, but more at the smell and feel of the masks. Their packaging, their marketing. This company is very on trend and the younger clients follow these trends. They don't want traditional oatmeal scrubs; they want grapefruit and mango." I explain to her for the hundredth time, knowing I'm wasting my breath.

Irene gives a sad little shake of her head "they don't know what's good for them, that's the real problem with these young ones." She picks up her paperwork and retreats to the back-kitchen area. The conversation is over. Irene would rather let the business go under than grow and keep up with the times.

ဆွာၐ

As I unlock the front door, Juliette greets me and helps with the grocery bags. "Maman, let me grab those and put them away for you." She entangles the plastic handles from my fingers and sets off toward the kitchen.

"You can leave the makings of the salad out, Juju, I'm going to make it straight away so we can eat before rehearsal tonight." I hope Marc will be home in time to join us, but if not, at least a salad didn't need any special keeping. He could just dish it up from the bowl when he got home. Since working things out with Gareth, Marc had been working more hours than ever. As he predicted, Gareth had begged him to come back and even offered a handsome raise. However, now I felt Marc was there more than before. I know he loves his job, but I am concerned it is cutting into our family time.

I quickly make the salad and call the kids to the table. "Maman, I got an A on my project today," Juliette's eyes sparkle and her smile beams at me proudly.

"That's fantastique, *Chérie*! I'm so proud of all the hard work you put into it." I don't think my little Juju has ever been graded anything other than an A. She puts her heart and soul into everything she undertakes and it shows.

I glance over at Olivier who is engrossed with his plate of salad, pushing a large crouton from one side of his plate to the other. I recognize his distractedness from when he was a young boy, trying to fade into the background, "what about you Olivier? Did you get your math test back yet?" Clearly, he's avoiding the subject of school as he pushes a slice of yellow pepper around his plate like a game of Pacman.

"Yeah, I didn't do so good." He looks up and meets my gaze. I raise my eyebrow questioningly, which sets him off with a list of excuses. "I can't stand Mr. Elwood, and I don't think I'm ever going to need to use logarithms or geometric proofs in the real world." He looks at me, imploring me to understand his point of view.

"Olivier, I understand you don't like those subjects, but you still need to do well in them for your overall mark." He nods, reassured that I'm not mad. "How bad is it?" I'm almost afraid to ask, but I know deep down I need to push him to do better or he'll coast along, too laid back. He is without doubt, his father's son.

"I got a 65%. Add that to my two previous tests this term and I'm averaging around 70%." His attention is back to moving the pepper around his plate, deflated and disappointed.

"Just a small improvement on each future test will bring you over the 75% into a potential B instead of a C. Why don't we make a plan for that to happen? Maybe even a little tutoring, yes?" I look encouragingly at Olivier and he lifts his head with a small smile.

"Thanks, Maman, you're the best." He gives me a hug as he sets to clear away his dishes from dinner.

Juliette clears the rest of the dishes, "go get ready for rehearsal Maman, and I'll tidy this up." I smile my thanks and head upstairs to get ready.

Within 10 minutes, Olivier and I are in the car and on our way. We arrive just in time for rehearsal.

"How many times have I asked you not to touch your hair, Lexi?" Catherine is standing in front of her car in the parking lot, working her daughter's hair into a high, tight ponytail. The poor child's face grimaces with every brush stroke.

"Evening Catherine," I call out to her. I know she'll hate to be caught fixing Lexi's hair in the parking lot like the rest of us common moms, she's too perfect for that.

"Hi Monique, Olivier, how are you both this evening?" her manners forcing her to respond to my jibe. I give her a little thumbs up and walk inside to the hall, quietly chuckling to myself.

"Maman, did you say that on purpose? That's not very nice." Olivier scolds me and I do my best to look chastised as I meet his glare. We both burst out laughing and I head over to our usual table.

Charlotte is fixated on her phone and doesn't notice my approach. She looks up as I pull out the chair beside her. "Charlotte, how are you today? You look very serious." Her face instantly relaxes with a wide smile.

"Monique, thank goodness you're here. Linda was over here trying to arrange a play date for Grace and Reese. I've been pretending to be busy ever since. She actually commented on how quaint it was that I brought coffee to our little club!" Clearly Linda had ruffled Charlotte's feathers. Not a difficult task, I might add.

"And then what, Charlotte? You felt bad for not inviting Linda to the table? For not having a coffee for her? Well, sweetheart, she has been sitting on her own at these rehearsals for years and you know why? Because she competes with the other moms and kiddies. She tries too hard, and she makes other people

54

feel like crap. That's on Linda, Charlotte, not on you. You can't fix everyone and everything." I rub her shoulder reassuringly. I know she means well but there's no point stressing over someone like Linda, you will never change that type of person. She slides me a coffee and I take a gulp. "Oh, you've already prepared it for me," the smoothness of the brandy is just what I need after my frustrating day with Irene.

I fill Charlotte in on my job at the salon and my struggles with Irene. "That's why you always look so good." I think Charlotte has been trying to guess what type of job I have. Little does she know, I dressed like this even when the kiddies were just babies and I stayed home with them. I would greet them at their cribs in the morning, with my hair styled and my makeup done. So many North American women failed to recognize what us Europeans already knew. Looking good on the outside, promotes feeling good on the inside.

"Hey Steph." Charlotte greets her as she sinks down into the chair opposite me.

"Hey girls. Char, you really are a lifesaver with this coffee. I'm beginning to look forward to Tuesday and Thursday evenings now." We all nod in agreement. I look around at these two women, who I have absolutely nothing in common with, and feel my heart warm. In such a short time, I have already grown so fond of them. It was strange really, being an immigrant, I didn't have large groups of friends like many other local people. I was grateful I didn't have to pretend to still like the people I went to high school with, or pass the time with small talk and pleasantries to people I no longer wanted to associate with. I had made Mom friends over the years through Olivier and Juliette, but I knew those women saw me as stand offish and a bit snobby. Just because I didn't show up at the school gates in my PJ's, I was somehow an elitist! Marc and I had a few couple friends, but as we've neared our forties, more than half of them have separated. On their kid-free weekends, they are living it up and partying like young singletons. We have drifted apart, with very different goals and interests. I didn't realize I needed these women, these new friends, until I found them.

"What's got you smiling, Monique?" Stephanie gives me a little nudge and I laugh.

"Just feeling grateful to have met you two ladies." I feel a bit embarrassed to be such a softie. The two of them 'awwwh' back at me in agreement.

"Can I have the attention of all the parents please?" Michelle is looking over at our table in particular. Rumbled again! "Next Wednesday, I am looking for volunteers to craft some props. From seven until nine, I am grateful to anyone who can come and help out. The crafts will be simple with full instructions, so no excuses," she laughs, "there will be pizza and drinks. It's a great opportunity to meet the other parents and get to know each other."

I hate crafting. I smooth down the silk sleeves of my blouse, just the idea of glitter and glue making me feel untidy.

"I feel as a new mom, I better offer to help."

"Of course, you do Charlotte!" I refuse to meet Stephanie's teasing glare and am surprised when I hear myself say, "why don't we all come together? I haven't helped for a few years now, so I also feel I'm due a turn. What do you think, Stephanie? Will you join us?"

She upturns her hands in a helpless gesture, "what kind of drinks will there be?" Ten years my junior, the newly single Stephanie has her priorities to think about.

I roll my eyes at her, "probably coffee and juices but I think sometimes she brings wine."

"I'm in." she announces which sets the three of us off into a new round of giggles.

"So, Steph, how are you doing? Any updates on the offer from your husband yet? Did you see a lawyer?" Charlotte has clearly been worrying about her.

Stephanie pulls a plastic binder from her handbag and slides it towards us. "This is the offer he's proposing. He says, it's the fairest he can offer. Unfortunately, I know the kids and I can't survive on that, so I've booked an appointment to see a lawyer on Tuesday. I've also dropped my resume off at a few local bars and restaurants. I used to waitress years ago, and I was thinking I could work every other weekend when Nate has the kids, to help top up his maintenance payments." Clearly, she was making great headway and planning for her future. I felt overcome with pride for her.

"You are doing amazing, Stephanie. Any restaurant will be lucky to have you. I'll keep my fingers crossed that you get an excellent lawyer who can work out what's best for you." I wonder if Marc's friend, Bernard, might need someone at the Bistro and I make a mental note to ask Marc to enquire on her behalf.

Charlotte interrupts my thoughts as she chuckles and we look over at her, "I was just thinking Steph, your milkshakes, would definitely bring all the boys to the yard." She guffawed. Uptight Charlotte really loosened up with a drink. We join in her laughter as we gather our things and make our way to the sign-up sheet, to volunteer for the craft evening.

"Awh ladies, you're all signing up for the crafts. That's wonderful, you'll be able to meet all the other parents too." Michelle smiles at me. "Monique, I thought you were allergic to crafting?" She challenges.

"Yes Michelle, I am, but these ladies are my armour and I am going to dress special for the occasion." Many of the loitering parents join in on the joke. I will come in the perfect outfit and show them all I could craft and be a mess with the best of them. "You will all see, maybe I will come in my PJ's and surprise you all." I threaten them. As their laughter increases, I give a wave of my hand and head off to join Olivier who's waiting at the entrance for me. I'm still smiling to myself as we reach the car. It feels good to be having fun. To join in on the camaraderie. To have girlfriends once again.

Stephanie

3rd Tuesday

I feel like I'm in a time out. In the corner of the office next to the Ficus plant, waiting to be summoned by Mr. Lynch, family attorney. Their office had some excellent reviews online, and their website stated they have a department that focuses on family law. So, with nothing to lose, I was here for my free consultation. I hope they don't keep me waiting much longer, I've sat here too long looking at my scuffed boots and I am now working my way up my pants, spotting loose threads.

"Mrs. Finch? Ms. Lynch, will see you now." The receptionist motions for me to follow her through the heavy wooden doors that separate the waiting area from the offices. Did she say Ms. Lynch? I thought I had booked with a Mr. Lynch. It doesn't really make a difference, but these are the days where I think I'm unravelling; when I can't remember the small details.

The receptionist gives a light knock on the door and pushes it open. I recognize the woman approaching me with her hand outstretched, but I can't remember where from. "Catherine Lynch, nice to meet you." I shake her hand as I realize, she's one of the theatre Moms. Her smile doesn't quite reach her eyes. "I'm sorry my father isn't here today, as planned. One of his clients has an emergency court hearing that he needed to attend, so I've stepped in for your consultation." She's mistaken my surprise to see her as disappointment that her father has not attended. She clearly doesn't recognise me.

"Err, no. It's fine, no worries." I take the seat she gestures for me, and fold my hands in my lap to stop myself from twiddling my fingers nervously.

"So, Mrs. Finch, why don't you tell me what's brought you here today." She is straight to the point and matter of fact. I don't know what I expected, but it wasn't this. I guess I thought I would pour my heart out and she and I would bond, becoming great friends, but my illusions ended right there.

"Please call me Steph," she nods. "My husband, Nate, has recently left, and he has approached me with a proposal regarding our finances. We have 2 kids and I don't work, so I'm not really sure what's fair or what I'm entitled to. I have updated my resume

61

and will start looking for a job this week, but in the meantime, I guess I thought I'd better get some advice." I'm out of breath. I'm babbling. Embarrassed in front of this formidable woman to be such a mess.

Catherine looks up from her note taking, as though she's seeing me for the first time. "Thank you for sharing all of that with me Stephanie, I am sure it's not an easy time for you right now." Oh no! She's being kind. No. I do not want kindness. Go back to mean, unapproachable Catherine, immediately. Kind Catherine is going to make me cry and I do not want to cry. I want to be brave and strong.

"Firstly, I want to reassure you, it's my job to ensure you get everything you are entitled to. Enough to provide a safe and stable home for you and your children. Anything you confide in me is of course confidential, but I will use the information you provide to our best advantage." Her soothing tone shocked me. It was so unexpected from her austere business-like manner. "I have a few questions here that I like to go through with new clients, to get a more general picture, and then I'll answer any concerns you might have. Is that ok?" I nod my consent, answering yes or no to the long list of questions she directs at me.

As she jots down my answers and writes side notes in the margins, I study her more closely. Her focus and concentration are powerful. I can already see her commitment and concentration on my case.

She puts her pen down and lays out her hands, palms up on her desk. "Now Steph, what questions do you have?" she smiles encouragingly, and I realize there are a lot of concerns I need answers to. Will I have to move? Will I be able to keep my kids with me on their birthdays and holidays? Can I stop Nate introducing every floozy he dates to them? Will I feel this broken for the rest of my life? With every new thought, my knee shakes a little more until, finally, the floodgates open and tears stream down my cheeks. Catherine slides an open box of tissues towards me and I grab one, hastily wiping the tears from my face.

"I'm sorry, I don't even know where to start. Every single one of my questions is based on Nate. I'm realizing that I'll be negotiating with him for the rest of my life and it seems so unfair after everything he's done to me." I wish I could explain my fears more adequately, but I don't have the energy to even try.

Catherine writes a few more notes. "Well Stephanie. It sounds to me like you have already been living a life on your husband's terms, and that hasn't worked out very well for either of you. It's my duty to make sure that your future can be as much on your terms as possible. My responsibility will be to negotiate for you. My commitment, to defend you. It's my job to protect you, and I take my job very seriously." I believe her. She has summarized my marriage in moments, and I am reassured that she'll be fighting my corner. Her no nonsense business approach is one of the few things I feel sure about right now. "Do you mind if I glance at the proposal Nate has offered you?"

I pass her the folder and she skim reads the document. Her brow crinkles across her forehead as she turns the first page. Her mouth twitches, and she bites down on her lip in an attempt to control it. As she finishes the last page, she holds it in the air and rips it into pieces, allowing it to fall onto her desk. "I'm going to go out on a limb here and guess that Nate is not a decent human being, Stephanie. He has clearly asked a lawyer to formulate this agreement to appear as if it's a simple arrangement, when in actual fact, this document is encouraging you to give up many rights. I'm not sure what kind of attorney would assist him with such underhandedness, but you certainly won't be accepting any of these terms." The determination in her voice released a fresh set of tears, but they were no longer tears of sadness, they were tears of relief. Catherine was going to help me. This tough, no nonsense woman was going to speak up on my behalf. For the first time in weeks, I didn't feel so afraid.

She asks me to return the same time next week for a full meeting, where she can begin outlining our proposal to Nate. She informs me not to converse further with him, unless it's about Lucy or Liam. I agree and thank her profusely as I leave the office.

As I walk out into the chilly afternoon, I take in a deep breath of fresh air and smile. Maybe, just maybe, I'm gonna be ok.

On our way to rehearsal, I swing by the doughnut store. I feel bad that Charlotte is always the one to bring us coffees, but I also sense that she likes her role as provider and caretaker. I don't want to step on any toes, but I'm pretty sure doughnuts are always - appreciated.

Throwing my scarf over the doughnut box discreetly I enter the hall. I feel guilty now, arriving with doughnuts for us adults when there are over fifty kids in the room. I make my way to our table at the back and place the doughnuts on the chair beside me, out of sight.

"Ohhh, naughty Steph, what have you brought us." Char spots the box before I even sit down.

I sssshh her, "I'll take them out in a bit when no one is looking." I glance around. Absolutely no one is interested in what we are doing. We laugh, and I fill the girls in on my visit to the lawyer's office, while we drink our coffees.

"She just ripped up the proposal?" Char asks again, in awe.

"Well, only the last page where I was meant to sign. Nevertheless, it was very impactful." I glance over to where Catherine is seated on the other side of the room, at her makeshift office. Completely immersed in her work, she appears oblivious that anyone else is around. No wonder she hadn't recognized me!

Monique nods her head in agreement, "I have heard she is one of the best in her field. I cannot believe I didn't think to recommend her to you, but I'm very glad you found her on your own, Stephanie. It was meant to be!"

Char leans forward and whispers, "I thought you said she was one of the perfect moms, looking down their noses at us?"

"No, that's Linda and Sandra. Catherine is just aloof. Like, she's too severe and professional." Monique is quick to explain.

Jotting away on her pad, she gives off a very 'do not approach' me vibe. "Honestly girls, she was magnificent. Very feisty, but also kind and soothing. I really felt she understood me, and wants to screw Nate over as much as I do." I laugh.

"I'm so happy, you've found someone to fight hard for you, Steph. I hope she gives Nate everything he deserves!" Char gives me a big smile, and motions her hand to the box on the chair beside me, "how about we celebrate with those doughnuts?"

I slide the box on the table and open its lid, discreetly as possible. The girls ooh and aah over the contents. A double chocolate filled Oreo crumble, an apple pecan traditional strudel, and a chocolate dipped in vanilla with toasted coconut, are nestled in the box. "These are not doughnuts, they are gifts from heaven," moans Monique as she bites into the gooey centre of the Oreo one.

Char wipes the sides of her mouth with a napkin, but misses the coconut flakes dangling from her chin like whiskers. "Where did you get these, Steph? They are simply divine!" The flakes fall from her chin as she's talking, and I regret not having grabbed my phone to capture a quick picture of her. The always together, organized and controlled Charlotte with her coconut beard!

"It's the new bakery on Front Street, called *The Patisserie*. An older woman, called Sabine, just opened it." I'm not going to share that I've already been there 3 times since it opened last week. I mean, it is important to support local business though, especially new ones.

"Well, I will definitely check them out. Thanks for letting us know." Char was already searching for it on her phone, saving the details so she wouldn't later forget.

"Ok Ladies, I need to leave early tonight, I am having dinner with Marc, but I will see you all tomorrow for craft evening, yes?" Monique slips on her grey woolen coat with a black fur trim and ties it effortlessly. She looks fabulous. I was slowly accepting that she always does. I have completely forgotten about volunteering for tomorrow night!

"Yes! We'll be here," Char answers for us both. "enjoy your romantic meal." She winks at Monique who sashays off, giggling like a schoolgirl. Olivier discreetly leaves the boys' group and joins his mom at the door, and I give them a wave as they leave.

I raise my eyebrows and purse my lips as I look back at Char. "Ok Steph, spill. Did you forget about craft night tomorrow? Or do you not want to go? What's up?" She's very intuitive. Even before my face pulling, I think she sensed I was in a bind.

"I forgot and haven't organized anything for the kids. I guess I can ask Nate if he can have them, but I wanted to follow Catherine's advice and only allow him visitations when he requests them."

Char pulls out her phone and taps a message. As she puts her phone down, I hear mine 'ping'. "you'll do no such thing. I've just sent you my address. Bring Liam and Lucy to my place tomorrow and Grace will mind them for you. Don't worry, she's excellent with kids and they'll have their own craft fun while we're out."

"Wow, are you sure?" she always finds a solution to any problem and makes it sound like it's no imposition at all. "Maybe

I'll pick them up some doughnuts," I think out loud, imagining which dessert I could tempt myself to try next.

"Whatever you need Steph, ok? Monique and I will be here to help and support you and the kids. You've got this and you're not alone." I'm blessed to have run into this bossy woman in the parking lot, only weeks ago. She barely knew me, but was supporting me as though we were childhood friends. I wipe a forming tear before it even has the chance to escape the corner of my eye and smile my thanks at her.

Lucy and Liam bound over to our table, looking questioningly at the empty box at the table. "Hey guys, great rehearsal! I could never imagine you would sound so good already," I smile proudly at them. Lucy's eyes shift from the box back to me and she lifts her eyebrows in demand of an explanation. "Hey guess what? Tomorrow you're gonna get to hang out with Char's daughter, Grace, at her house. She's gonna craft with you while I come and help here with the crafting night. If you're really, really good we will stop at the new bakery on the way and grab a treat for each of you, deal?" I offer them.

"Deal." They reply in unison, eager at the thought of a visit to the new bakery. We wave bye to Char and Levi as we make our way out to the parking lot. The air is mild for a winter's evening. I unlock the car and settle in with the kids, I look at each of their happy, rosy faces and for the first time in weeks, I feel content.

The Unicorn Moms

Just in the present, not worrying about tomorrow, or caring about yesterday; just living in the moment.

Charlotte

Craft night

Is there anything better than laying on the couch and having your feet massaged by the man you love? I sink further into our oversized cream couch as Adam works the arch of my foot, releasing all my inner tension. I hear Grace's melodic voice singing, as she completes the after dinner clean up. This has always been my dream. A husband, kids, and a happy life. I see other women my age, who hanker after career goals and status symbol cars, but I don't think those things make you truly happy.

I was successful in my younger life, before Adam and the kids came along. I was always fighting to stay on top and compete with my peers. It was hard work and draining. At the time I thought I was just competitive and liked to win, but now I'm older

I can recognize it for what it was. Loneliness. I didn't have a family to rush home to. I didn't even have friends, just colleagues who I was friendly with. People who would buy you a drink at the bar but you wouldn't invite them home. Most of those years were spent networking in clubs and hotel bars, and if I'm truly honest, I have only vague recollections of those years. I worked hard to keep busy, and drank to avoid the loneliness. Often times, I think Adam coming along saved my life.

Sometimes I forget I was ever that person, but when I remember, I am thankful to have evolved. To be this better version of myself. Charlotte 2.0

The large farmhouse style clock on the wall chimes; it's 6:30pm. "I need to freshen up." I smile at Adam.

"Can't you just skip it? I mean, are you even good at arts and crafts?" He's teasing because he knows I can't handle the mess of crafting. The idea of glitter everywhere, never to be fully eradicated, has put a ban on crafting in our house, with the exception of the basement workroom. He tickles my feet. I wriggle and squirm to get away from him.

"Adam, stop it! I'll pee my pants and I won't be laughing." I chastise him.

That just seems to encourage him even more. "Well, I'll be laughing enough for the two of us, so don't you worry." He grabs a tighter grip around my ankle and runs a light finger up and down my foot.

I jerk and buck like a penned in horse. I wrangle my foot loose and narrowly miss kicking Adam in the face which only sets him off laughing harder. I often wonder if Adam is a little sadistic. He loves causing trouble and being naughty. "That's it, you're grounded." I inform him as I straighten myself off of the couch.

"Ohhh, will I need to sit in the corner or on the naughty step?" His handsome face looks serious as though pondering his fate, but his tone is silly and playful. "Maybe we should work out the details more specifically when you get home?" He winks at me.

I shake my head at him as I leave the room to get ready. Secretly, I would love to miss this crafting evening. It will be full with the other judgemental moms, and I can already feel the impending stress settling in. However, I would hate to show up and for Monique or Stephanie to desert me, so I'm not going to do that to them. Plus, Gabrielle will make it tonight and I can introduce the other girls to her. I finish tying up my hair in a high pony and smile into the mirror. Nothing like a super tight updo for an instant mini face lift. I rub a gloss across my naked lips and grab my favourite pashmina off the chair by my vanity.

I stop by Levi's room on my way toward the staircase, "Hey, finishing your homework?" He's leaned over a workbook, doodling in the margins.

"Hey Mom, just finishing my project with Danny," He clicks his mute button on his headset, "have a fun night, love you."

I blow him a little kiss and make my way to the front door, just as the doorbell rings. "Steph, Liam, Lucy, welcome! Come on in." I usher them inside as Grace appears from the den.

"Hey Lucy, hi Liam, are you excited to hang out with me tonight?" Grace smiles at them. Liam tugs at his shirt a little nervously while Lucy beams back at Grace.

"We brought treats!" Lucy announces excitedly as she holds up a box from *The Patisserie*.

"Should we put them in the kitchen for now?" Grace asks.

"Ummm, ok." Lucy clearly wanted the treats now but Grace was right to leave them as something to look forward to.

"Be good for Grace guys, ok? We'll only be a couple of hours and I know she has some fun things planned for you." Steph reassures them as I grab my coat.

"Let's go into the den and see what I've got set up for you two, and don't worry Liam, if crafting isn't really your style, Levi said he can set up his game console for you." Liam's eyes light up as Grace leads them towards the den.

"Don't worry Steph, Grace is excellent with kids. They're in good hands, and Adam is in the living room if they need anything." I rub her arm gently. I can see she's finding it difficult to leave them.

Steph turns to me with tears in her eyes. "No, I'm not worried about them. I'm just so thankful. They've gone off happy and eager. I'm so grateful to you Charlotte, opening your family to us." She leans forward and hugs me. I can feel the weight of worry physically lift from her.

"Steph, you never need to feel alone or judged, ok? We've got you." I promise her solemnly. "Now let's go or we'll have Monique to deal with." I laugh, and she joins in. "Bye guys, I shouldn't be too long, love you's." I call out as we leave the house. I faintly hear 'love you's' in the distance and we head off into the night.

∞

As we enter the hall, I see 4 tables have been set up in the middle of the room. All pushed together with about twenty chairs around them. Almost half the chairs are already taken. I look towards Steph who nods back at me nervously. Maybe we should have arrived later, so Monique would already have chosen us a space. Now we were going to have to make uncomfortable small talk with these women, in the deafening silence.

"Hey Char, how are you my lovely?" I hear a voice behind me and turn. Gabrielle kisses me firmly on the cheek and I introduce her to Steph. "Steph, I'm delighted to meet you." Gabrielle turns on her 1000-watt smile as she guides us toward the end of the table and some empty chairs. "Hello ladies, I'm Gabrielle and these are my friends Char and Steph, we are delighted to join you all this evening." I see the women around the table taking in their first impression of Gabrielle, and I lower my chin to hide my smirk. Uncomfortable silence does not affect her. The world is her stage and the rest of us are her audience. She has a confidence us North American women simply can't pull off, without coming across as snobby or downright rude. She's dressed simply in workout leggings, with a chenille striped sweater. If I wore her outfit, it would look drab, lazy even, but Gabrielle's body sets the outfit on fire. The leggings made her butt look perkier than ever, and the hint of cleavage in the v neck of her sweater was hard not to catch. I can never quite figure out if it's her physical body as a personal trainer, or her Brazilian confidence, but she just oozes sensuality. Almost like you feel sinful taking her all in. She smiles at each of the faces as they introduce themselves to us, and I know I won't remember any of their names so I don't even try.

We settle in our places as Monique arrives. She grabs the chair opposite us and I make the introductions. I watch as Monique takes in Gabrielle. I'm almost positive these two women will become great friends, but equally wary they might dislike each other on first site. Too similar, but different. I'm trying to think of a topic they'll both agree on when Michelle enters the room. "Evening ladies. Wow, so many of you tonight! Thank you so much, this will make our task a lot easier." She picks up a stick from her piano and glides towards our table. "So basically, we will turn these sticks into brooms for our chimney sweep number. The boys dance during this song, and at the end of the scene they throw the brooms into the audience, so we need to make sure they are attached securely. I've brought some fake hay and twine along with black cardboard, and I think we'll be able to make one prototype together and then all copy it. So, what do you all think?" She looks around at us all expectantly.

"Michelle, how about if we use the twine to wrap the hay around the sticks, trussing them, and then decorate the outside with thin cardboard strips imitating a dirty, used broom?" Linda is already cutting up strips as she speaks to demonstrate her idea. I can see why Monique has said she's annoying and tries too hard, but her idea seems good and saves the rest of us from having to contribute, so we all smile encouragingly. I catch Monique's subtle eye roll my way and do my best not to laugh. Unfortunately, Gabrielle also caught it and is giggling to herself like a child. I elbow her to stop and give her a stern warning look.

"Actually Michelle, if we rolled the cardboard in the center, and glued on pieces of blackened hay to the outside, I think they would look much more authentic." Sandra is hastily grabbing pieces of cardboard and folding them, arranging pieces of hay around it, smiling at everyone around the table with her 'better' version.

Steph snorts from her chair and quietly whispers to the rest of us "Oh God, we have a craft off." All 4 of us look away from each other, and I bite my tongue in an effort to not burst out laughing.

Michelle smiles and invites us to help ourselves to coffee or wine, which she has set up in the corner, while she looks at Linda and Sandra's prototypes.

Steph is up and out of her chair in a flash and the first to pour herself a glass of Rosé. She hands me a glass as I approach the table. "Thanks Steph, just what I need." I take a large swig from the plastic cup and pass it back to her to top me up before the others join us.

"How many glasses of this will I need in order to complete this craft?" Monique enquires as she approaches us. Steph laughs and hands her a cup filled to the brim.

"There isn't enough here, Monique, for any of us to care as much as those other Mom's." Steph laughs and we join in.

Gabrielle grabs a bottle of water and heads back to the table. She's not a drinker. You only have to look at her perfect skin to see she would never dehydrate it using poisons such as alcohol. Her body is her temple. Admittedly, if my body looked like hers, I would probably treat it more respectfully too! In our youth, I used to think my drinking would eventually push Gabrielle away, but through the years, even some of the rougher ones, she has always encouraged and supported me, even if she hasn't exactly agreed with my behaviour.

Michelle has worked out a prototype from the two suggestions and demonstrates to the room how to assemble the broom. We collectively set to work, cutting strips of cardboard and fraying hay edges.

There's general chatter around the table about tv shows and recently read books until Steph loudly stage-whispers, "Hey girls, I've joined a dating site." Her exuberant confession has brought the room to deafening quiet and we all look at her expectantly.

I can see the redness from her chest working its way up her neck to her face, realizing too late, that everyone has heard her.

"Don't keep us in suspense, tell us more." Gabrielle dramatically pleads, and the other women 'hhmmm' in agreement, nodding their heads encouragingly at Steph. This was another of Gabrielle's gifts. She could turn the most awkward moments normal; her eager, smiling face, encouraging everyone else to be just as kind and just as open as she is.

"Well, as some of you know, my husband has recently walked out on me." Frowns and looks of concern cross the other women's faces, as Steph begins her tale. "It's ok, I'm slowly coming to terms with the fact that he was a piece of shit." She smiles at Catherine, at the far end of the table who is listening wholeheartedly. "Well, anyway, he's now shacked up with his new girlfriend and I thought two can play at that game, but it's not as easy as it looks. Dating has really changed since high school." There are nods and murmurs of agreement around the table. "So, I signed up for 'Queen Bees', which is a site specifically for divorcees, and I thought it was going so well when I received numerous matches and invitations to chat. Half the invites were bogus and trying to get me to sign up for a premium chatline, and the other half were weirdos sending me pics of their little man." She recounted to the table at large.

"Did you just say little man?" Monique laughed. "Is this what you call a man's dick? Little man? This does not bode well for your husband's new girlfriend." There's a silence around the table. The other women are shocked at Monique's brazenness. Steph laughs hysterically and we all join in until there are literal tears streaming down her face.

"You have to persevere. I'm sure once you wade through the scam artists and weirdos, there are still some decent men left out there." I don't want Steph to give up just yet, her self-esteem needs this validation right now. Gabrielle nods in agreement.

"You don't need Mr. Right, anyway, you just need Mr. Right now." She arches her eyebrow and the table sets off in a new round of laughter.

We continue to laugh and joke easily through the evening, and after an hour we have completed 28 brooms. Steph is taking turns riding some of them around the room while Monique is pretending to sweep up. "We need to ensure they're sturdy and fit for purpose." Monique informs the rest of us. The majority smile back at her high jinks with Steph, but I can see Linda and Sandra are very focused on finishing their final pieces. They have contributed little to the conversations throughout the evening, and I have no doubt they'll be recalling our outlandishness to their husbands when they get home. The rest of us clean up and put all the craft supplies back in the tote Michelle brought them in. Steph and Monique gather all the brooms and ask Michelle if she would like them brought out to her car.

"Oh, that's ok ladies, I'm gonna keep them here for when we get closer to dress rehearsals. I can see by the way you've product tested them though, that they'll do the job nicely," her eyes twinkle at us and I'm relieved she's enjoyed our fun and jokes. She comes across as a little austere, but I'm pretty sure it's just a front. I should know, I have the same mechanism.

We place the brooms behind a wall divider near the stacked chairs, and prepare ourselves to leave.

Catherine approaches our end of the table as she buckles her Donna Karan down-filled jacket. "Steph, I admired your bravery to share all of that with the rest of us." She pats Steph's arm as Monique, Gabrielle, and I look on astounded. It seems Catherine wasn't as cold or judgemental as she appeared. "I'll see you next rehearsal. Goodnight all." She calls out to the room at large.

"Yes, I'm off too, g'night ladies." Monique waves as she makes her way to the door.

"You sure you're ok, Steph?" I want to reassure myself she wasn't just putting on a brave face. If I don't ask her outright, I won't sleep tonight, wondering if I should have said something. Anxiety really is a devil to live with on a daily basis. Steph nods and smiles at me. She's ok, she's stronger than we think.

We wave bye to the others and walk with Gabrielle towards our cars. "I had such a fun night tonight, ladies. Char, you were right, these new women are lovely. I'm glad I came and met them. Do you think you would all like to come to a yoga night, if I organize it for you? No charge of course." She's always encouraging me to relax more.

A feeling of love fills me, and I smile at her. "I'm sure everyone would love it, thank you, Gabrielle. I'll make a group text and see what dates might work, ok?"

"I definitely could do with working out a bit more." Steph agrees. "I've gotta keep in shape in case I get any dates." She laughs easily.

"Sounds good, let me know what works for you all" Gabrielle unlocks and opens her car door. "*Tchau*", she calls as she closes the door with a little wave. I start the Jeep, barely able to hold on to the ice-cold steering wheel. "A remote start is what I need for this bloody car. I love it but it's so cold." I can see my breath as I complain to Steph. She has her arms tucked under her armpits across her chest.

"Honestly, you do. My boobs are frozen." She confesses and we laugh the entire ride home. As we push open the front door, laughter echoes through the house. "Sounds like the kids are having a great time with Grace, thank you so much, again." Steph is relieved they're having so much fun. We follow the sounds and find Lucy, Liam, Adam and Grace all playing Wii Bowling.

"Mom, look, I'm winning." Liam proudly announces to Steph as we enter the room. "Also, we played Just Dance and I can't wait to show you the videos I took of Adam and his moves." He laughs.

"That's awesome buddy, I'm so glad you had a great time. Now let's get going and let Charlotte and Adam have their quiet home back." Steph ushers the kids to the hallway and we all sing song goodbyes.

"Drive safe guys, thanks for coming." I wave out the door as their car reverses onto the street. "Grace, thanks so much for showing those kiddies such a great time, I really appreciate it."

"I had a lot of fun with them and Steph gave me this, so it's a win-win." She holds a $20 note between her hands as she winks at me.

"Goodnight Grace, love you." I call as she heads upstairs. I return to the living room to deal with Adam and his punishment from being naughty earlier. A slow smile creeps across my face in anticipation as I close the French doors behind me and announce, "who's been a naughty boy then?"

Monique

3rd Thursday

It's only 11am and already the day is dragging on. We have no more clients booked in for the rest of the day and the place is already spotless. I'm not really feeling well. Maybe I should go home at lunchtime? Despite there being no bookings and no chance of walk-ins, I know Irene will not be happy with me if I leave.

"Monique, I have a meeting today, will you be all right to take your lunch at 12?" Sometimes I think she can actually read my mind. If she wants me to take lunch at twelve, then she must want to go at one for her meeting. I might as well be stuck here until three.

"Sure, Irene, no problem." I respond cheerily. I really am part of the problem. If only I stood up to her. Forced her to see the inevitable doom of failure ahead if we don't somehow revive our little salon. Truth was, I didn't want to destroy her illusions. I didn't want to be the person to shatter the hopes and dreams she had spent her whole life working towards. The day of reckoning was not far, however, and I really needed to start looking for a new job. Just the idea made me feel like a traitor to poor old Irene.

I put on some pop music and sweep the floor. Might as well keep busy.

At twelve, I grab my coat and head out to *Es-presso*, our little coffee shop. I order two coffees and a grilled cheese to take back to work. It's cold and windy. I rush back with my head bent down, out of the wind. As I enter the foyer, I hear Irene's voice, "there's also an apartment upstairs, with a separate entrance around back." Her voice is coming from the hallway which leads to the 2 private treatment rooms. I leave Irene's coffee by the front desk and head to the kitchen.

I can still hear the muffled voices, but I can't make out what they're discussing. The second voice is deep. Why would Irene be giving some man a tour? I finish my sandwich and tidy up the little kitchen. "Ouch," I've snagged the edge of my nail and go to grab a file from the manicure station.

"Thank you so much Ms. Bronner. The office will schedule the photographer as soon as possible and be in touch." The suited forty something gentleman is shaking Irene's hand as she positively beams back at him.

I file my nail edge and wait for Irene to finish seeing her guest out the door. "Monique finished lunch already?" she brazenly challenges me. I look at her expectantly. Is she really not going to explain our visitor?

"Just fixing a nail. Who was your guest, Irene?" I can hear my tone is accusatory, but I'm mad that she's forcing me to use bad manners by not having introduced me.

"Oh, Jeremy is the real estate Broker who is going to help me with the sale of the business." She replies flippantly.

"Have you decided to sell The Village Spa?" I'm dumbfounded. Did she decide to sell the business without even letting me know? I must be jumping to conclusions; there's no way Irene would make such a gigantic decision, without having the minimum courtesy to let me know.

"Over the last year Monique, I have been listening to you. It has been hard to accept, but I admit you are right. The salon is no longer making money, and we have fallen behind our competition. Today's younger people are not looking for wholesome and healthy treatments. They are looking for gimmicks. I am losing money on a weekly basis and have finally decided to sell the business while there is still something left to sell."

Oh no you don't Irene. You are not going to make out like this was all my idea and advice that I gave to you. How dare she? "Irene, my advice was for the Spa to evolve and for us to move ahead with the times, not to give up. I have worked here for the last ten years and I can't believe you've reached this monumental resolution without even consulting me." I am incensed that Irene thinks so little of me.

I need to get out of here before I do or say something I may later regret.

"Monique, you are one of the best technicians I know, you will find another job without any problems." Her reassuring tone just aggravates me further. She is following me around as I collect my things.

I open the front door and I turn to her, "I can't believe you Irene. I have had many opportunities over the years to move on, but I have always stayed loyal to you, to our friendship. I can't believe this is how you're repaying me." I shake my head at her and slam the door behind me. I can hear her calling out after me, but I'm not interested. I yank open my car door and drive home. The journey is filled with head-shaking, and white-knuckle steering-wheel gripping. Anger and disappointment take turns flowing through my veins.

I enter the house and drop my things on the hall table. I dial Marc's cell phone, but there's no answer. I wonder if a bath will diffuse some of this anger? I draw a bath, grab my robe, and drop a fizzy lavender bomb into the bath as I step in. I allow the warm water to soothe my muscles, and try to relax my whirling mind. Tears pour down my face and at last I let go. The tension, the disappointment and hurt hit me all at once. How had I let this happen? How had I waited for life to just pass me by? I'm 45 years old and unemployed. This is not how I imagined my life would turn out. I will never regret having put my duties as a wife and mother before my career choices, but I thought I would have made something of myself and my skills by now. The realization that I had sat back and let opportunities pass me by hit even harder than Irene's low blow.

I drain the bath and wrap up in my plush robe. I apply moisturiser to my tear-stained face, and lay back on my pillows on the bed to meditate for a few minutes.

I can feel a hand gently jostling my shoulder. "Hey Monique, are you ok?" Marc enquires, as I open my sleepy eyes and peer up at him. I remember my morning, and falling asleep on the bed. The sadness floods back and my eyes water. "What is it? What has happened, *Chérie*?" He gently coaxes the details out of me. Even as I recount the story back to him. It seems surreal.

"No wonder you are so upset. Irene should be ashamed of herself to treat you with such little consideration. I'm proud that you walked out of there, you showed her!" Marc is fired up on my behalf, always my protector. He settles on the pillows next to me and I snuggle into his chest. Nothing else really matters. As long as I have Marc, we will deal with whatever else life throws at us. "Why don't I heat up some chicken soup and put a movie on the laptop here for you?" Marc offers.

"I don't have much of an appetite, to be honest, I'm not really hungry." I feel bad, I know he wants to do something to help me.

He reaches over to his bedside table and offers me a thinly rolled joint with a smile. "This will help you relax and solve your appetite problem, you see, medicinal purpose only, Monique." I shake my head at him.

I'm not averse to the odd toke to help me sleep at night, but it was too early in the evening for me. "I still need to take the kids to rehearsal." I small sigh escapes my lips.

Mary O'Hora

Marc lifts himself from the bed and stands over me, "I will not hear any more nonsense from you, Monique. I will take the kids this evening and you will stay home and relax. Watch a movie and let us take care of you for a change." I can feel the tears sting my eyes as gratefulness fills my heart. I know many women who have amazing careers but unhappy homes. How lucky I am to have Marc and our kids to look after me. I take his outstretched hand and follow him downstairs to our garage couch.

He lights the twisted paper edge and passes me the joint. As I inhale deeply, I hold the smoke for as long as I can, willing the cannabis to work its magic and relax my mind as quickly as possible.

Marc tucks a throw around my legs and sets off to make me some soup. After a few more puffs, I stub out the joint and leave it in the ashtray for Marc to finish later. I make my way back to my room while I still have the energy to move. "Juju sweetheart, what are you doing?" Juliette has lit several candles around the room and is setting up the laptop on the wooden fold-out table, set out on our bed.

She pulls back the corner of our pintuck silver duvet. "Papa has told me about your crappy day, so we are gonna pamper and treat you to a relaxing evening, Maman. Hop in," she pats the mattress and again, I am reminded how blessed I am. I slide into the sheets and give Juliette a hug to thank her for her kindness.

"Madame, dinner is served." Marc appears at the doorway balancing a tray filled with goodies. He sets it on my bedside table and I feel my appetite growing.

I look at the never-ending offerings on the tray, I know there's no way I will finish all of this. "Marc, there's way too much food here, I will never eat all of this." I explain as I pick up a thin slice of brown bread smeared with brie.

Marc dismisses my protests with a wave of his hand. "I'll finish whatever's left when I get back from rehearsals, don't you worry." He leans down and kisses my forehead. "Try to relax Chérie, ok?" He encourages. I nod my agreement, afraid to speak in case my voice cracks. Juliette leans over and presses play on the laptop and I give them a small wave as they leave, softly closing the door behind them. I roll my eyes as I recognize the opening scene from Pretty Woman, and settle back into my pillows to escape reality for an hour or two.

ৎ৶৶ৣ

The room is dark, I must have dozed off during the movie. I check the time on my phone and notice I have 3 notifications. The first message is from Irene. **Monique, I'm sorry if today came as a shock to you. You've been warning me for years and sadly I didn't listen. I don't have the energy or desire to salvage what little is left of the business, and it has been a very traumatic decision for me to reach this conclusion. Please do not think that I did not take you into consideration. I recognize, in my grief, I failed to deliver this news to you appropriately. I hope this will not damage our friendship irreparably, and I urge you to come in on Monday so we can work out the finer details. Love, Irene x.**

I felt bad for her. She had been hiding from reality, and I can only imagine how devastating it was to arrive at the decision to sell her livelihood. I would message her tomorrow and agree to go in on Monday to talk things over.

Hi! I saw your kids arrive with a gorgeous hunk of a man who I can only presume is your hubby and so I just wanted to check you were doing ok? There's a lot of colds going around at the moment, so please let me know if you need anything at all, ok? Of course, the ever-caring Charlotte would wonder what's wrong when I didn't show up at practise. I'm surprised the girls didn't force Marc to sit with them. I chuckle to myself, imagining the stares Marc would get from some of the mean moms. Luckily, Juliette had gone with him to keep him company.

I hope it's ok to message you, I spoke briefly with Marc and he let me know you've had a shitty day. Over the last few weeks, both you and Charlotte have been a great support system for me. If there's anything at all I can do or if you just wanna talk or even not talk. I'm here anytime. The final message from Stephanie, filled with care and concern. Not only do I have a great family, but I have made some really sincere friends amongst these ladies.

I hear the truck reverse onto the drive, and the bustle of the kids and Marc entering the front door. My bedroom door creeps open slowly as Olivier peers in. "I'm awake, sweetheart, come in." I gesture the space next to me.

"Are you feeling better Maman?" He asks, as he switches on my bedside lamp.

I wipe the sleep from my eyes and take in my handsome young son. Concern etches across his face. He is worried for me, not used to his Maman taking to her bed for the day. "I'm already feeling much better." I reassure him and he leans in to hug me.

"Olivier, let's go. Teeth brushing and pick out clothes for the morning, please," Marc glides trough the room and flops onto our bed. "I've missed you," he smiles as he grabs my hand. "Your gal pals cornered me and insisted I join them at their table about halfway through. They arc incorrigible Monique. Also, someone should teach that Charlotte one how to measure a shot of brandy.

I'm not sure there was even any coffee in my cup." He laughs as he recounts the evening and his first impressions of the girls to me. I'm happy he got good vibes from them. Maybe he would get along with Adam? Although, I struggle to imagine what type of man had taken on Charlotte for all these years.

"I'm gonna check the kids are getting ready for bed and I'll be straight back to discuss your new opportunities."

I don't have the faintest idea what opportunities he's referring to. "What are you talking about?"

"For years I have encouraged and urged you to leave that parlour behind, but you were always too loyal, too faithful to old Irene and her outdated ways. Finally, the Gods of fate have spoken and are offering you the chance to change the future. If that's not worth being thankful for, then I don't know what is." Wow, Marc is right, I have turned down offers in the past and they will appear again. I need to focus on the positive outlook and stop being such a negative nelly.

Stephanie

4th Tuesday

I pull down the visor over the driver's seat and give my appearance a final once over. Not too bad Steph, force a small fake smile and you'll be just fine.

Going in for my interview at Doyle's now, wish me luck. I send the message in our group to Monique and Char. I exit my car and walk towards the Irish bar that sits, overlooking the river, downtown. They're not actively hiring at the moment, but an old high school girlfriend set up an interview for me with the bar Manager Matt, who is her cousin. I open the heavy oak door and enter the dimly lit bar area. A young server approaches me, "Welcome to Doyle's, are you here for food or a drink at the bar?" He enquires pleasantly.

"Hi, I'm Stephanie, I'm here to see Matt." I feel self-conscious and I just know my chest is turning bright red. Some aspects of anxiety you just can't hide.

The server smiles at me and gestures to a nearby booth. "Get yourself settled in and I'll let Matt know you're here." He saunters off towards the back of the bar. I remove my coat and slide onto the bench. I hear my phone ping and quickly put my hand in my bag, reaching for the switch to put it on silent mode.

I smooth out my blouse and fold my hands in my lap, attempting to look poised, but feeling anything but. "Stephanie, I'm Matt, pleased to meet you." He says as he slides onto the bench opposite me. His dark hair falls in tendrils across his forehead. His stubble is groomed perfectly. It looks effortless, like maybe he just woke up like this, but I would bet money on it necessitating a close trim every day to keep it looking so perfect. He's dressed in a casual chic style. Designer jeans teamed with a dress shirt and several top buttons left undone, revealing his manscaped chest. He had wound a bandana through his hair, allowing the front half to flop forward. I could imagine many a single lady sitting at the bar, just to watch the eye candy. "I hope my cousin, Jen, let you know that we aren't actually in need of anyone right now, but we do sometimes need people on a call-in basis. If that might work for you?" I nod in agreement. "Great, so have you worked in bars and restaurants before? Tell me a bit about yourself and what previous experience you've had." His warm hazelnut eyes look at me, encouragingly.

"I'm going to be completely honest with you, Matt. I've been a stay-at-home mom for the last twelve years. However, before my kids, I used to be a server at Magnolia's, and I tended bar at The Locomotion back in the day." I smile at him, hoping my eager friendliness will make my outdated experience seem more relevant. "I totally accept that the till systems and even drink recipes have changed in all those years, but I am a really quick learner. Could I possibly shadow another staff member, unpaid, until I get the gist of it?" Oh God, I'm grasping at straws and I sound desperate. I will myself to shut up and meet Matt's gaze. He looks amused. Great, I knew I had made a complete idiot out of myself!

He slides some forms and a pen towards me. "Listen Steph, I've been managing this bar for over 5 years and Jen has never asked me to see anyone on her behalf. I know she doesn't vouch for people normally, and her recommendation is good enough for me. I know you will need some training sessions to bring you up to speed, but I can see you're eager and willing. In this industry, that's already half the battle. Fill out all your details here and I'll ask my assistant Rebecca to schedule you in for some initial training shifts. How does that sound?" It sounds bloody wonderful. I can feel grateful tears working their way to my eyes. I smile and nod as I pick up the pen. Thankfully, my hair falls to the side of my face and shields my watery eyes. I bite my bottom lip hard to allay any tears, and concentrate on filling out the paperwork. Once complete, I double check the info and hand the papers back to Matt. "I really appreciate this opportunity, Matt. I won't let you down." I assure him.

He smiles back at me, "I think you'll be a great addition to our team, Steph. Rebecca will call you tomorrow with training dates and to arrange picking up your uniform." He stands up from the booth and I follow suit. I shake his outstretched hand and feel the smoothness of his skin.

"Great, again, thanks so much!" As I reach the door, I half wave like an over excited schoolgirl, and he nods back. God, I am embarrassing sometimes. Silly or not, I've got a job, and it's a start. I pull out my phone as I enter my car and I see two notifications. Both are from the girls. Char's reads, **You've got this Steph! Sending prayers!!** And Monique's is typical. **Break a leg...... get in the cast!** Followed by ten heart emojis!

I type out a new message to my old friend, Jen. **I got the job! I could tell your recommendation held a lot of weight in this decision. Thank you so much for believing in me and vouching for me, You're the best!** I press send and within seconds my phone pings back. **I knew you'd be the perfect fit, congrats!** Feeling super proud of myself, I decide the kids and I should celebrate with a treat. I navigate my way to *The Patisserie* to pick us up a little something for after dinner.

૭৵৵

80s hits are blasting through the speaker when Liam and Lucy come through the door. I've tidied up and prepared some hot chocolate bombs to go with our treats from the bakery. "Hi Mom," Liam calls as he kicks off his winter boots, and leaves a trail of his outerwear on the floor in his wake, rushing to the downstairs bathroom.

"Guess what, Mom. I won our history bingo today, and I got to pick from the rewards drawer and look what I got." Lucy is holding up a pink pencil with a troll head topper. Its fiery pink hair has been swooped upwardly. She beams at me proudly.

I stoop down and inspect her prize, "she looks just like you, Lucy. Messy hair, don't care." I laugh as I tousle her very own bird's nest, which has formed under her winter hat.

She puts her coat and bag away as I pick up Liam's discarded items off the floor. Within minutes they join me in the kitchen, looking for an after-school snack. "Ooh, who are these for?" Lucy spots the hot chocolate bombs and treats from *The Patisserie*.

I retrieve 3 of my favourite winter tartan mugs from the cupboard. "They're for us," I smile at them, "we're celebrating."

"Is dad coming back?" Liam asks excitedly as he returns to the kitchen. My heart crashes to the pit of my stomach. Of course, the kids will not see my new job as a celebration. They're going to see it as a step further away from the only life they've ever known. I feel sad that in my own disappointment and hurt, I hadn't really accepted the kids are not yet ready to move on.

I join them at the breakfast bar and rub Liam's shoulders. "I'm sorry, Honey. No, your dad is not coming back, and if I'm going to be absolutely honest with you, I wouldn't want him back. He's a great dad to you, but he wasn't a great husband for me. I really think that once we adapt to our new way of life, we will all be happier, even daddy." I force my voice to sound as positive as I can. "I'm here to answer any questions or worries you have, ok? I know I won't always have the answers, but we will work them out together as a family." Despite myself, I can feel the tears burn my eyes. Both kids look back at me, sad and scared. I wrap an arm around each of them and slowly they both hold on to me and cry.

"Mom, Lucy's snivelling snot into your hair," Liam chuckles, but his voice cracks from too many tears. Lucy and I join in his laughter.

I stand upright. "C'mon, let's wash our faces and enjoy some hot chocolates." I scurry them out of the kitchen and take a baby wipe to my patchy pink face. I boil the milk and set out the mugs with each hot chocolate bomb on a side plate. I fill two serving dishes with marshmallows and sprinkles. I grab the can of whipped cream from the fridge and place it between our mugs. Liam and Lucy return, and each grab a seat beside me. "So, watch me do mine first, and then you can do yours ok?" They nod in agreement. I pop the chocolate bomb into the mug and drizzle the boiling milk from the gravy boat that I've used as improvisation. The milk hits the chocolate, and it dissolves, releasing the powder from inside. Chocolate and powder swirl together with the milk, and it is mesmerising to watch. As the milk reaches the top of the mug, I add some fluffy marshmallows. I grab the can of cream and squirt a generous amount on top of my creation. A few sprinkles on top and it's done.

I look at the kids as I bend my head to take a first sip and their eyes are wide with excitement. "Me next, Mom. Please, is it my turn?" Lucy can no longer contain her anticipation. I glance at Liam, who nods. I knew he would let Lucy go first. Always the generous and giving older brother to his younger eight-year-old sibling.

After our hot chocolates, I rustle up a quick chicken fajita dinner while the kids do their homework at the kitchen table. We voted to save our pastries until after rehearsal, as an evening snack.

I put on some easy listening music in the background and hum through my chores.

♔

In the car, we sing along to the radio on the way to rehearsals. I see their brief glances in my direction, worried they've hurt my feelings with thoughts and wishes about their dad. I smile at them in the rear-view mirror, and sing even more ridiculously to reassure them I'm ok. I'm strong; I'm their Mom. "Hey Mom," Lucy calls out from the back seat, and I lower the radio sound to better hear her. "What were we gonna celebrate earlier, anyway?" she asks.

"Oh, it was nothing really. Just that I got a job today." My tone is apologetic. I don't want my babies to be scared, I don't want them to worry.

Liam leans forward and squeezes my shoulder. "That's not nothing, Mom. That's awesome, where is it?" Trust my caring

Liam to support me, even if it's taking a step further away from our old family life.

"It's just a casual job at Doyle's, but it's a start." I grin at them, feeling silly to be so excited about such a minor accomplishment.

"Will we get to eat there free now?" Lucy wants to know. I shake my head at her and explain how we might get a discount, but definitely not free food. I reassure them both that I'll mainly work when they're with their dad, so it won't interrupt our family time. "It's ok Mom, Liam can look after me if you have to work. He's old enough now and I promise I'll be a good listener so you won't need to worry about us."

I feel an overwhelming urge to hug her. "That's right, Mom. Lucy and I will hold the fort at home whenever you need, so you don't need to let your new boss down." Liam agrees.

I'm blessed. Nate may be a lying, cheating scumbag, but these amazing kids make everything worthwhile. "It's my job to look after you two and I love it. Don't grow up too fast," I mockingly wave my finger at them as I pull into an empty parking space.

We get out of the car and walk towards the hall, hand in hand. Just before the entrance, Liam gives my hand a little squeeze before he lets go to run ahead and join his friends.

As we enter, Lucy also skips off to join her group. I smile at Catherine as I walk past her makeshift desk, and she lifts her head and responds with a brief wave. I join Charlotte at our usual table. "Steph, how was the job interview? When will you hear?" I love how genuinely excited for me she is.

I grab the seat next to her and give her a powerful hug. "I got the job! Thanks for all your prayers and encouragement Char, it truly means so much to me." She squeezes me back tight.

"That's marvellous, I am delighted for you."

"I am going to guess that you got the job, Stephanie?" Monique has correctly evaluated our hugging scene. I turn to her, nodding. "That's fantastique. I knew they would hire you, who wouldn't want a beautiful, talented server like you?" She bestows her brilliant smile on me.

"How are you, Monique?" Char asks her gently as she takes the seat opposite us. "We missed you last week. Although, I will admit, it was fun to put your hubby under pressure in your absence." She smiles at Monique.

"Ladies, thank you for your kind messages. I am doing so much better. I went to the salon yesterday and cleared the air with Irene. I can see she thinks she's doing the best for the salon. She's kind of hoping the new buyer will want to keep it as a going concern, but one look at the books will put an end to that pipe dream. I will look for another job soon, but I have promised Marc to take a little time and decide what I really want to do with my future. He wants me to accept this as an opportunity to see the world as my oyster, but honestly, I think I'm a bit old for a new start." I can see it's hard for her to admit this to us.

"Well, I for one think Marc is absolutely right. The world is your oyster, Monique. So many salons would jump at the chances of hiring someone as experienced as you." I reassure her.

Char nods in agreement. "you'll land exactly where God intends, you'll see." Char chimes in.

"Thank you, ladies. I sure hope you are both right. Anyway, Stephanie, apart from the job, what else is new? Any more dates I need to hear about?" She asks me pointedly.

I fiddle with my hands in my lap unsure how to confess to them, I am too scared to go on any 'real' dates. "I have been chatting with a few different guys, that don't seem to be complete pervs, but I don't think I'm ready to meet in the actual, real world yet." I admit to them.

"Nonsense." Char cuts me off "You need to get back on the horse," she informs me.

Monique agrees with her, and the two of them bombard me with questions about why I haven't set up a date yet. "When Nate left, he said he was driven to cheat on me because of me and my flappy bird," I whisper to them without once looking up or meeting their eye. The feelings of inadequacy quickly engulf me, and I feel the stinging of tears yet again.

Char looks baffled, and Monique looks away from me. "Your what?" Char clarifies.

Monique's shoulders shake and I hear a tiny grunt escape her lips. She turns back to face us, unable to contain her amusement. "Her flappy bird." Monique quietly shrieks to Char and dissolves into hysterics. Char looks from me to Monique, clearly caught between sadness and laughter. As her body slowly shakes, it becomes apparent she is joining Monique in her mirth.

"Girls, this is totally not funny." I look at them, hoping they can understand. "I feel very self-conscious now. I've never been concerned with things like this before, but now I'm paranoid. What if there is something wrong with me?" I plead with them to see how tragic and important this is.

"Oh Stephanie, you are perfection. That coward of a husband simply used these insults as an excuse for his appalling behaviour. Clearly his little man was too small for the job." She sets off into a fresh round of giggles and Char joins in. I realize how ridiculous I was to ever listen to anything Nate had to say.

I look at both of my new friends, their faces pink from laughter, and Char asks, "Is that an actual saying though? Flappy bird? I'm very behind the times." I shake my head and the ridiculousness of it all hits me. Laughter overtakes me as Linda at the next table 'shhhh's' us, which only causes us to laugh harder.

Gabrielle

Yoga night

I mark a small cross in the dough sitting in the loaf pan, and slide it into the oven. I push the timer and start tidying up the ingredients still out on the counter. Max will be home soon and I want to have dinner on the table early, so I have plenty of time to get ready for tonight's yoga class.

"No, don't slide forward until you hear the change in music." Adriana's voice echoes down the hallway, and I hear a loud thump followed by Karla's deep laugh. "Ok, next time don't lean forward as much. Get up, let's try this again."

"Alexa, play Ibiza jams." Some dance music will drown out the girls. I imagine they're making videos, but I don't have the time to distract myself with their games. I really need tonight to be a success. It will be the first private session that I've held as an instructor at The Lotus, and I finally have a chance to make some extra money for myself. For four years I've helped Christopher run his classes, while I've obtained my different diplomas and certifications, and I am now ready to make a name for myself. I have my regulars, but they pay memberships to attend my classes. Even though I have the most participants in my class, I'm still paid the same flat rate fee.

During my apprenticeship, Christopher devised a rate to pay me per class, but that was 4 years ago. Now I am fully qualified, and he still pays me the same. When I broached the subject with him recently, he explained that sadly The Lotus wasn't making enough to increase my class rate, but I could borrow the upstairs studio, three evenings a week, if I wanted to make some extra cash. When I first met him, he only had 30 members, but now we have grown that number to over 120 people who pay $29.95 per month. I get paid $35 per class and I take anywhere between ten to fourteen classes a week. I also cover a majority of Christopher's classes at the last minute when he has errands to run or appointments to attend. He never pays me for covering for him, and recently I've started to feel unappreciated. I even man the front desk in between my scheduled classes for free. I'm hoping my drop-in evening Yoga sessions at $8 per person will really take off. If nothing else, it will allow me to see if there's room for me to branch out on my own.

Max and I certainly couldn't afford to lease a studio, but if these sessions go well, I could use it as a bargaining tool to negotiate my next position at another fitness studio. "What's cooking Mom, it smells so good," Adriana is a foodie. "Is it cheese bread?" Her nose has guessed correctly. *Pao de Queijo* is one of the girl's favourite Brazilian treats, and I try to incorporate it into our meals at least twice a month. It's a simple enough cheese bread recipe, and it evokes memories of home.

"Yes darling, I have made a prawn salad and I thought we would team it up with the bread to make a healthy, easy, dinner." She's listening as she scours the pantry. "Adri, we're eating in about 15 minutes, please get out of there, and why are you still in your uniform?" The girls attend Mount Carmel Catholic School for girls. It's a forty-five-minute drive away, but they have a bus that picks them up locally. It's an expensive outgoing in our budget every year, but Max and I want the best for them. Growing up in Piaui, Brazil, I was no stranger to poverty, and although Max grew up here in Canada, his single Mom had to work three part-time jobs just to make ends meet. We were both adamant that we would make sacrifices now for the benefit of our girls' future.

Lola jumps down from her raised dog bed, where she had been sleeping, and dashes to the front hallway. "I guess Daddy is

111

home." I laugh with Adri. Lola is our little Pomeranian, and she can hear as soon as Max's old truck turns down our street. Max bought her for me for my birthday last year. He thinks I am struggling with separation anxiety as the girls are getting older and needing me less. I just wish the time would stop going by so fast. For the record, I think Max babies Lola even more than the girls and I do. I think he is the one with separation anxiety about the girls. I smile to myself as he enters the kitchen.

"How was your day?" I ask him cheerily.

He reaches me and kisses me tenderly. Max thinks couples who give each other a peck on the cheek take each other for granted. He says he never wants to forget the desire he felt the first time he kissed me, and so needs to remind himself daily. He's a silly old romantic, but I will admit, I always try to look my best for him. Adri climbs onto the side of the armchair to sit close to her dad. "Oh, it was a relatively easy day. Mike and I got the capping on Mr. Grutes roof finished, so we're on schedule to start that house on Lakeshore next week." Max owns his own roofing business, and although it's only a small local company, he always has work lined up. People know he prices fair and works hard, two difficult tasks in manual labour.

"I have my first Yoga class tonight, so I've just made a quick salad and cheese bread, I hope that's ok." I gesture to Adri to lay the table and I check the rolls with a long toothpick. "Slightly damp, give me another five minutes and it will be ready."

Max inhales exaggeratively, "smells amazing to me. I'll just get out of these overalls and freshen up."

He stands and squeezes Adriana's knee just in the right spot, making her jump. "Dad, one day I'm gonna get you back, then we'll see." She warns him. I smile at her as I hear Max chuckling up the staircase. I set out a bottle of beer for him, he's not a big drinker but does enjoy a drink with dinner. Adri makes chocolate milk for herself and Karla, while I cut a few slices of lemon and lime to add to my carbonated water.

છ∞જી

I arrive at The Lotus way earlier than I needed to, but I am eager to set things up just so to create the perfect atmosphere. There will be 12 of us this evening. Charlotte is bringing the new moms from the theatre group with her, and my online ad brought in the rest. I turn on the lights at the back of the studio and the small pot lights at the front, but I leave the main overhead lights turned off. Christopher has this room over lit during his Yoga sessions, and I always feel it takes away from the overall relaxing feel that should be created.

I place a few of my Ylang Ylang and Jasmine candles around the room and light them. Their subtle scent helping to create the perfect atmosphere. I take our largest mats out of the closet and make a pattern laying them out on the floor. I want to create a sense and feeling of calm for everyone from the moment they enter the room. Having to grab their own mat and then decide in a room of strangers where to place it, and how far from each other, gives me a feeling of anxiety that I certainly don't intend to bring into my classes.

I put out 6 bottles of water on the front table, in case anyone has forgotten theirs. On each mat, I place a fluffy hand towel with a trial tube of my hand and body lotion. It's my unique creation: a mix of mandarin, spearmint, juniper, and orange oils to invigorate the mind and body. One day when I have my own studio, I will offer my own natural products. Over the years, as a hobby, I've created face masks, lotions, exfoliants and gifted them to friends. I just need to be in the right place, at the right time for all my hard work to pay off. I know one day my turn will come, and when it does, I'll be ready.

The stereo system in the studio is too powerful, designed more with Zumba and bootcamp classes in mind. I switch off the main speakers, and leave on only the small ones around the perimeter of the room, at a low level. I have to strain to hear the soothing music now, but once we're all in place and focused, it will be exactly at the right volume. I walk back out into the hallway, and re enter the room with fresh eyes. The scene that greets me is one of calm serenity. The subtle lighting and the low music instantly sooth my mind.

I hear chatter in the foyer and go out to meet my first clients. "Hi, I'm Gabby, are you here for the yoga class?" I smile at the three women in front of me. They nod and smile back. Two of them are much younger than the other but they all have similar features. I would guess they were mother and daughters. The older one fishes out her wallet. "Shall we pay you now?" I walk behind the counter to grab a receipt pad as the door chime announces more arrivals.

Over the next 5 minutes, I take everyone's payments and invite them to find a comfy place in the studio at the end of the hall. Everyone but one person has shown up, which I know is great for drop-in classes. I feel excited and proud as I join the rest of the class. I enter the room and at once realize my preparation had all been worth it. No one is aimlessly chatting or looking at their phones. Some of the women are lying down and doing breathwork. Other are trying out a small amount of hand cream, massaging it into their hands and arms. I have created the perfect elusive atmosphere.

"Thank you all for joining me this evening for our very first Yoga drop-in session." My voice is almost a whisper in the silent room. "I am not sure how many of you have attended Yoga classes before, but I also mix in a bit of meditation in my sessions, so I hope this new experience will be one you will all enjoy. We will learn many yoga positions today, but I don't expect us to master any of them. Yoga is a constant growth, so please don't worry yourselves with how you look during this class, but only with how you feel, ok? Unlike many other workouts, the art of perfecting the moves will improve over time, but the mental benefits can be felt immediately. So, I urge you to open your mind and be prepared to really let go." The room full of faces smile back at me eagerly, and I sit myself down, on my mat, at the front of the class.

We start with some basic stretching exercises and I introduce the group to some beginner poses. I hear a few giggles from Charlotte's group, as we focus on the cat and cow poses, but overall, the group of women seem to enjoy the experience. I finish our session with some slow stretches and a five-minute mini meditation. I am encouraged when I call the session to an end and notice none of the women move right away. All too relaxed, they slowly gather themselves and their things.

"See you next Wednesday, Gabby." The group of three call out.

"Well, I wasn't sure Yoga was for me, but I really enjoyed this. What did you think, Lily?" I overhear a lady say to her friend.

I feel warm inside. The evening was a complete success. I wave goodnight to the rest of the ladies, and return to the studio room to blow out the candles. Christopher would not be pleased if anything was out of place upon his arrival tomorrow. As I enter the room, I notice Char and Monique are putting the mats away, and Stephanie is blowing out all the candles. "Ladies, that is so kind of you to stay and help me." I tell them, gratefully.

"Nonsense," says Monique, "even when Marc has taken me for a luxury spa weekend, the classes are not as good as this one. $8 is a gift! I hope that's not your regular price Gabrielle. I would expect to pay at least $20 for such a session elsewhere." Steph and Char nod their agreement.

I feel blessed to have such support, and proud my work is finally paying off. "Thanks, Monique. I must keep my prices low if I want to grow a following, but one day I'll be able to charge more. Maybe when I join a new studio, if I find one upmarket enough." Christopher's studio was on the wrong side of town, and unfortunately, the 'ladies who lunch' would not travel south of the highway to attend any classes here.

Char closes the closet door. "Anything else you need help with, Gabby?" she asks, as she puts on her coat.

I look around at the perfectly clean room and shake my head. "Nope, I'll just lock up and set the alarm once I see you all out." I smile my thanks at all three of them.

"I think we should have a little treat," Stephanie chimes in. "*The Reverb* down the street serves the most amazing martinis if anyone wants to know." I decline the invitation, and the three women set off towards the bar. I watch as they link arms down the street. I'm happy Char has made some new friends, but I hope she doesn't fall into old habits, trying to fit in with everyone. I noticed at the craft night, she downed two glasses of wine in succession. She's come a long way since our college days, and worked hard to be on good terms with alcohol. I hope she's watching herself.

I lock up and make my way home. My heart is full, and I hope my Dad in heaven is looking down at me proudly. Far from the state of Piaui and the poverty I left behind in Brazil. My hardworking dad had worked relentlessly to give me the opportunity to come to college in Canada, for a chance at a better life. Within the first year, I had met Max and fallen pregnant with Adriana. I always felt my dad may have thought I had thrown his sacrifices away, but here I was making something of myself. I knew he was cheering me on from the clouds above.

Charlotte

4th Thursday

I can't move my head. My eyes feel glued together, and my mouth feels like sandpaper. I try to turn over and pull the covers over my head, but my churning gut lets me know there's no way I get to go back to sleep right now.

My stomach grumbles and I feel the nausea rising. I drag myself off of the bed and make my way to the bathroom. My legs won't cooperate. As I bash my thigh into the bedside table, I collapse to the floor. I crawl the rest of the way to the bathroom, and say a silent prayer as my clammy hands hold on to the toilet bowl. Not again, God, please not again.

လွှာ

"Mom? Mom, are you ok?" I can hear Levi's voice, and feel my arm shake, but I don't want to wake up just yet. Waking up will bring consequences, and I just can't cope with that right now.

I turn away from Levi. "Mmmm, I'm fine honey, just a little ill today, maybe a bit of flu." I murmur, hoping it's enough to send him away.

He rubs my back, "we both know it's not the flu, Mom. You need to get in the shower, you have throw-up in your hair. If you're in bed when Grace comes home, it will give her a fright. Please clean yourself up. Not for mine or your sake, but at least for Grace." He walks out of the room and as I hear the door softly click. Humiliation overwhelms me. Here I was doing exactly what I had promised myself I would never do to my children. I can't even remember how I got to bed. I had promised Adam after the last time that if I ever black out again, I would stop drinking once and for all. I reach for my phone, there's an unread message from Adam. **Char, I hope you're feeling ok when you wake up. We need to talk this evening. I'll pick up take away on the way home**.

Dragging myself into the bathroom, I turn on the shower. I eye myself up in the mirror and I am shocked at the reflection staring back at me. My face looks grey and gaunt. Deep bags hang under my sorrowful eyes. Oh my God, my hair! Levi wasn't exaggerating. It's matted together with what looks like sick. I can't even remember how I got into this state. I enter the shower and let the heat pulse my body back to life. Shame, disappointment, and bewilderment join me as tears flood my face. How have I gotten here? What's happened? Cool, controlled Charlotte. That's who I am, not this raging mess. I turn the water temperature hotter and hotter until my skin burns and I can't feel it anymore.

Like an out-of-body experience, I watch myself, fumbling to wash my tangled disgusting hair. I drop the soap twice and eventually grab Adam's body wash, too frail to bend down to pick up the soap again. I towel off and dress in joggers and an old, oversized t-shirt. I attempt to brush my hair, but my head hurts so bad I just tie it up in a messy bun. I need to take something for the pain, but I also want to feel this pain. I don't want to allow myself to shirk this off. To make like it didn't happen. If I grab two aspirin in the kitchen, with a shot of brandy for medicinal purposes, I'm sure I'll be as right as rain by the time Adam comes home. As I watch myself return to my bedroom, I plead with myself to make the right choice. I pick up my mobile and dial.

"Dr Kelsey's office, how may I help you?" Thank goodness it's Marcie who answers.

"Marcie, hi, it's Charlotte. I need an appointment, please." The shakiness in my voice is undisguisable.

I could hear her flipping through pages. "Of course, Charlotte, How's Monday at 2:00pm, does that suit?" Shoot, I couldn't wait that long. A loud sob escapes my throat and before I realize, I'm bawling down the line. Explaining to Marcie that I'm not doing so good and don't think I can wait that long. "Char, come in at 4 and I will squeeze you in between two patients, ok? Will Adam bring you or will you need a ride?" Bless her, she had been on duty after my last episode. She knew I was back where I had started. I reassure her I will get a ride, and hang up. I return Adam's text. **I've got an appointment at four with the doctor in case you get home before me. I will make this right, Adam, I promise**.

I can't catch my breath. Anxiety engulfs and overtakes my body. There's a pounding inside my head, and I keep feeling cramps across my chest. Deep down I know it's merely a panic attack, but I'm scared. I lay out on the bed and attempt some deep breathing exercises. Guilt and shame mix with my fear, and I am convinced I'm experiencing a heart attack. I intake a large breath and hold it for a count of five. I continue repeating this process, right up until a count of twenty. The twisted knot of panic in my chest has eased, and while I still feel awful, I don't think I'm in any immediate danger. My phone pings and I read Adam's reply. **I will be home at 3:30pm to pick you up**. Even when he has every right to be mad and angry, he reaches out to support me. How could I do this to him? To Levi and to Grace?

I shakily make my way downstairs. The kitchen is clean, with no hint of last night's dysfunction. Levi is at the breakfast table, intently ignoring me. I grab two pieces of bread and pop them in the toaster. "Levi," I begin.

He stands up and looks straight through me, "Mom, please don't. There's nothing you can say or do right now. I can't even look at you." He wipes a tear with the sleeve of his shirt as he leaves me alone. I am disgusted with myself. The toaster pops and I butter the toast. It tastes like cardboard in my dry mouth, but I force it down. I know I need to eat. I check the fridge calendar, relieved that Grace has robotics club and will get the late bus home at five. I drink two glasses of water, hoping to help my dehydrated body, but the pounding in my head continues. I long to take some aspirin, but I know I need to feel the full effects of my decisions in order to make a change. I can't just pop a few pills and say it's fine this time. I've gone too far.

As I sit in the armchair by the patio doors, the sunlight falls on me as hazy memories of last night flood back to me. I had left the yoga studio so relaxed, and I had been so excited to go and have a few martinis with the girls. I remember getting a table at the bar, and laughing with Monique and Stephanie, but after that, nothing. I don't know how I got home. The rest of the evening is just a huge blank.

I hear Adam's key turn in the door, and I go to meet him. "Char," his voice catches and I can see he can't get his words out. Tears fill his eyes. I hate myself for making him feel this way. He opens his arms and I rush into his embrace. My body is racked with sobs and Adam holds me tight, reassuring me. "We'll find a way, we always do." He whispers, and I feel my neck wet with his tears. "Come on. Let's go see Helen." He ushers me to the car and we make our way to the doctor's office.

∽∾

"So, Charlotte, what's happened? What's brought you in today?" Helen Kelsey has been our family doctor since before either Levi or Grace were born. Over the years we have become friends. She was truly the only person, apart from Adam, who knew the depths of my struggles.

I look at her open, encouraging face and attempt to state my case. "I went for a few drinks with friends. I was excited and in good form. And that's it, that's all I remember. I know that can't be all there is because I slept all day, and at some point, I blacked out. I just don't know how I got this bad. I've been having the odd few drinks here and there for years now and I've been fine. I scrunch my eyes tight, unwilling to give into the threat of tears. I don't deserve tears or sympathy right now. I know I need repercussions. Something has to change.

Helen continues taking notes and raises her eyebrow at Adam, "is that it, Adam?" she asks him, pointedly.

"Uhmm, well more or less." Helen waits him out in the silence. "Well, Char went for Yoga at seven, and after to the bar for a few drinks with some of her new Mom friends. I know her anxiety escalates when she's with new people and that probably caused her to have a few more than she should have. She called me from the bar, just before midnight, because her car had broken down. Her friends had gone home, the bar was closing and she couldn't start her vehicle." Adam was looking down into his lap. I know he's embarrassed by my behaviour and having to be the one to call me out.

Helen puts her pen down on the pad beside her and removes her glasses. "Charlotte, I can see this episode has disturbed you greatly, and the admission from Adam that you were willing to drive in that state really points out how far things have escalated since last time we met. Your anxiety is affecting your everyday life. I know you like to be in control. I know you don't agree with taking medication, but your mental health is suffering. You really need some help and support right now." She looks at me intently. Her no-nonsense tone is letting me know these recommendations are not up for negotiation. I nod back slowly. "You could have woken in the ER this morning if your car hadn't broken down," she continued. "From our past interactions, it is clear that you are suffering from general anxiety disorder. I know you refute that diagnosis, but I am going to ask you to take a little leap of faith and give me one month. Take my advice and directions for one month and if you don't see some major differences, we'll reassess. Does that sound fair to you?" She looks from me to Adam, who is already nodding in agreement and reluctantly I nod my head. "Great. Now, I want you to have patience and give these pills a chance to work, ok? Most people feel a difference within 14 days. It is imperative that you eat and sleep well during this time to give the medication the best chance of success. I want you to fill your spare time with hobbies or exercise, so you have a task to unwind with, and projects to look forward to. Do you think you can handle all of that?" I sigh and nod. I feel Adam squeeze my hand and I meet his gaze. It's hopeful and supportive. I try and muster a smile to return, I know it's the least he deserves.

Helen completes the script and hands it to me. "40 mg of Prozac daily to be taken with food, no alcohol. These meds and alcohol don't mix well together so you need to lay off the booze, at least until the pills have some of the anxiety under control, ok?"

"Thank you, Helen. I'm sorry I've let it get this bad." I can't even meet Adam's look. My hair falls around my face as I bow my head, and my shoulders rack with the sobs that have broken through my dam of denial.

I feel like I have been holding my breath for the last two years. Trying to get it right. To be a good Mom and wife and not let my family down. It's over. It's time to admit I'm no longer coping, and my anxiety is slowly winning. I take a few deep breaths and stand. Adam takes my arm and leads me back to the car. I buckle my seat belt and stare aimlessly out the window.

Adam places his hand on my knee. "Charlotte Owens, you are not alone. We will support you through this." I turn to face him but my throat is closed and I cannot respond. Shame and disappointment won't allow me to speak. "You have been working so hard for years. Accepting help does not mean you failed. It means you are a strong enough person to get support, so you can be your best, for yourself and for our family. That is not failure, that is success, and I don't want to hear you say anything to the contrary." His tone is firm but the love in his eyes is unmistakable. I grab his hand and hold on for dear life, the entire drive home.

Monique

5th Tuesday

I pack the last of my mementos into the cardboard box on the manicure table, and take a last look around. I feel sad, like I'm leaving an old friend. The room is filled with so much unattained potential. Deep down, I guess I always thought I would convince Irene to keep up with the times, and the Spa would grow to reach its full potential. Maybe it still would, I simply would no longer be a part of the dream.

The building isn't sold yet. Irene wants to sell the place as a package, the building and the business, but has received no interest from any potential business owners. Only developers for the building itself. She has conditionally accepted a fairly low offer from a private party, but to my understanding, the finances were still being worked on. Irene was hoping to sell her business stock and treatments, but other salons have their own suppliers, and she has not yet received any offers. Marc has been trying to encourage me to buy some of Irene's stock and some fixtures to set up temporarily at home until I decide what I really want, but my heart isn't in it.

"Well, Monique, I never thought this day would come." Irene's eyes shine with un-spilled tears, and there's a soft tremor in her voice. I feel bad for her. I have Marc and the kids to go home to with their support and love until I figure out my next move.

Irene has only ever had this place. After her husband Alberto died, this building was all she had left. I think that's the real reason she has clung onto it for so long. The memories. "I know you're sad, Irene, but once the deal is complete and you're soaking up the sun in your new Floridian home, you'll forget all about us." I reassure her, teasingly. She was in the process of purchasing a luxury townhome, in a gated community, in Fort Lauderdale. I had seen the brochures, and it looked heavenly.

I fold down the lid of my box and place it by the front door. "Don't be a stranger Irene, you know where I am, whatever you need, ok?" She nods her understanding and throws her arms around me.

"I'm sorry it came to this." She sobs into my shoulder and I rub her back, reassuring her all will be well.

Maybe this would turn out best for both of us, who knows? I have to cling onto that hope. "We'll both end up happier in the end, Irene, you'll see." I let go of her and smile. "Call me if you need help boxing up the stock next week." I offer, as I pick up my box and open the front door. With a last glance around, and a wave to Irene, I walk out to my car without looking back. As I slide into the driver's seat, a small faint tear slips out of the corner of my eye.

ക

I pop the garlic bread into the oven, and set the eight-minute timer. I place the salad on the table and call Juliette down to lay out the cutlery.

"It smells so good, Maman." She sets the table and makes a carafe of iced tea for her and Olivier. I pour myself a glass of wine, and pass Juliette an empty wine glass to place at Marc's setting.

I hear the front door keypad beep open. "*Coucou,* I'm home." Marc's melodic voice sings out from down the hallway.

"We're in the kitchen." Juliette sing-song's back to him.

He enters, and wraps his arms around my waist. "How are you, Chérie?" His eyes look deeply into mine, searching to discover if I'm actually fine, or just pretending.

I nod and smile, reassuring him my feelings are genuine. "I'm ok. In fact, I feel better than I thought I would. Maybe it hasn't actually hit me yet." I reason.

"Or maybe you knew you were too good for that place and deep down know you need a new start?" Marc suggests playfully.

"Sure," I silence the oven timer and remove the garlic bread. I know Marc wants me to embrace the idea of a new adventure, and I am doing my best to keep a positive outlook. "Olivier, dinner time" I call out, hoping my voice will be heard in his room upstairs. The wheels of his gaming chair sliding across the room let me know he has heard me.

Once we're all seated, Marc says grace, and as I look around at my beautiful family, I know I'm blessed. A job is just a job, I'm sure I'll find another.

"To Maman," Marc raises his glass, and the kids and I reach in to clink our glasses.

They look at me hesitantly, like they expect me to start crying. "I'm fine, stop worrying about me. I'm excited for the new possibilities ahead." I lift a square of lasagna and serve it onto Olivier's plate. I serve Juliette and Marc before sitting back down with a serving for myself.

"This is really good Maman, thank you." Juliette reaches for a slice of garlic bread and passes the tray around to the rest of us. Olivier and Marc murmur their agreement. As I listen to the kids' chatter about their day, and Marc playfully tease them, I am grateful for this life we've built. Thankful for the love and support I have.

∽∾

"Stephanie, you're here first today." I smile, as I approach the table.

"Yeah, I wonder if Char is going to miss today's rehearsal as well. Have you heard anything from her?" I shake my head, wondering how Charlotte is doing. She hadn't responded to the text messages we sent in the group, and Grace and Levi had missed Thursday's rehearsal.

It seemed unlike Charlotte to not respond, and for the kids to miss any rehearsals. "I hope everything is ok. Oh, look there's Levi with the boys, maybe Adam dropped them off?" I wondered out loud. I scanned the room, but there was no sign of Adam or Charlotte anywhere. "How was your weekend, Stephanie? Have you had any of your training sessions yet?" I was eager to hear how the new job was working out for her.

She raised her eyebrows and rolled her eyes. "Well, I've had two sessions so far, and I can tell you things have changed a lot since I last worked a bar." She chuckles, and I settle more comfortably in my seat, eager to hear her latest tale. "So, on my first shift I managed to drop a tray full of plates, trying to navigate the kitchen's swinging doors." She spreads her arms wide to demonstrate the enormity of the mess she made. "The following session I forgot to charge a table for their drinks. Luckily, Allie, the girl I was shadowing, caught my mistake. If not, I would have had to pay the $28 out of my tips." Stephanie sighed and I could sense her stress at the situation.

"I can't believe if you make a mistake, you have to pay out of your own pocket." Of course, no one wants to make mistakes, but having to financially pay for them seemed very unfair to me.

Stephanie shrugged her shoulders, "I hear you, but back in the day I think everyone abused the system, and now with all the modern technology, they can make us individually accountable." She explains to me how ten years ago, people would visit her at work just to get a free drink added to their meal and it made her feel super uncomfortable. She was looking forward to being able to do her job without having to try to sneak in freebies to her friends. "Nate's been asking to see the kids every other weekend, so I will be ready to take some actual shifts soon. Catherine is working on our last proposal now, and I hope he's going to accept our terms and conditions or else we're going to court. She is great at what she does, I'm so glad I found her." The admiration in Stephanie's voice was palpable. I was also glad she had found Catherine. Her reputation in town preceded her. "Enough about me, how are you doing? Wasn't today the day you packed up your things at Irene's place?"

It was only earlier today, but in a surreal way it felt like it was weeks ago. "It was ok. Luckily our talk on Monday had cleared the air so that made it easier to go in for my final goodbye. In fact, I kind of feel sorry for Irene now. At least I still have a life at home. Work was all she had."

"Nonsense." Stephanie said. "she'll be living it up in Florida in no time, and you'll find the perfect job. You'll see."

I smile at her enthusiasm and hope she was right. "Oh, that reminds me, I've brought a few facial samples for you guys to try. I've left them in my car. I'll run out and grab them, be back in two mins." I grab my car keys off the table, and nip out to my car before she could even protest.

The wind has turned chilly. I rush to the trunk of my car and find the samples right away. As I close the trunk and hit the lock on my key fob, I notice a red Jeep parked two rows behind me. I could swear it was Charlotte's Jeep. I move closer towards it and I can see a faint light shining from inside. Once I'm in front of the vehicle, I can make out Charlotte's silhouette, illuminated by the light from her phone; she's watching something and doesn't sense my presence. I quietly step backwards and retreat back into the hall to rejoin Stephanie.

Her face looks at me eagerly, "Were they not there?" Her left eyebrow lifts with her voice tone. My face must look bewildered as she continues, "the samples, Monique! Isn't that what you went to your car for?" She laughs at my forgetfulness. I pull the sample packs from my cardigan pocket and pass them to her. "Oh, wow! These are amazing, thanks so much." She continues, oblivious to my distraction.

"Stephanie? When Charlotte and I happened upon you in the parking lot, do you sometimes wish we had left you alone?" I ask her cautiously.

She looks up from the sample packs and cocks her head to one side. "Well, that's a bizarre question, but yes I guess I wished you had left me alone. Now that I know the two of you, I'm grateful, but at the time I was very embarrassed." A light pink flush rises to her cheeks as she recalls the memory. "Why are you asking about that, anyway?" She's curious.

"Well, I saw Charlotte's Jeep outside, and she was in it, watching something on her phone." I confide to her.

Her face is bewildered. "Maybe it's her husband, Adam, in the Jeep. Perhaps he's waiting for Levi and Grace?"

I shake my head, "No, I went right up to the Jeep, it was her." I bite the corner edge of my lip. I'm worried about our friend.

"Well did you speak to her? What did she say?" Stephanie wants all the details, but I have none to give.

I lay my palms up on the table. "I backed away, I didn't want to embarrass her. If she doesn't want to be seen, I don't want to force her." Stephanie pushes her chair back, picks up her coat, and heads for the door. "What are you doing?" I'm trailing behind her, trying to catch up.

"I'm going out to check on Charlotte. You guys don't get to witness me wailing in my car for me not to return the favour. You were both there when I needed you, and now we're gonna do the same for Char, whether she likes it or not."

She strode towards Charlotte's red Jeep, like a woman on a mission, and I felt fiercely proud of my young friend and the strength she has gained back in the last few weeks. Tap, tap, tap. She rattles on the driver's side window.

Charlotte jumps in her seat as she turns and spots us peering in at her. She pushes the button to wind down her window. "Sorry ladies, I've been so poorly all week, didn't want to get you ill as well." She smiles weakly at us both.

"Oh, Charlotte, I am so sorry you're not feeling well, is there anything we can do for you?" I ask gently.

Stephanie walks around to the passenger side and is pulling at the handle, motioning for Charlotte to unlock the door for her. As the car unlocks, she slides into the passenger seats and motions for me to slide into the back. Once in the car, she turns to meet Charlotte in the eyes, and flat out asks, "so, what's really going on?" I can see Charlotte about to protest, but Stephanie's death stare causes her to waver.

Her eyes cast down into her lap, and as she lifts her head to meet our questioning gaze, I notice tears threatening to overspill onto her face. "I'm sorry, I've been a bit of a mess. Since getting trashed the other night at The Reverb actually," She sniffs back her tears.

"Charlotte, are you in this state because you got drunk, let loose a little and now have a shame hangover? We all have nights where we let ourselves relax a bit too much. We're not here to judge, are we Monique?" Stephanie nods at me and I assure Charlotte we are here as friends, concerned for her.

Over the next half hour, Charlotte confides in us the stresses she's been dealing with recently, and her fear about her mental health. She tells us this has happened before in her youth, but the last incident was over two years ago, and she really felt she was doing better now. "What if I have to be on these pills forever?" Her voice cracked, as she admitted her deepest fear.

"Charlotte, everybody is getting help somehow. Whether it's the young Mom with the au pair, or the Dad who has a few drinks in the garage in the evening while he tinkers around." I reassure her. "Is the new prescription helping?" I enquire.

She nods, "Well I definitely feel less worried, but I've also been hiding, so I guess it's really too early to tell." She explains sheepishly.

I nod my understanding. "Is Adam ok? Is he supporting you and helping you?" I know she's probably trying to shoulder it all on her own, but I hope she's letting her family help.

She reassures me instantly that Adam and the kids are supporting her. I can tell she doesn't want us to worry about her.

"Listen Char, if you and Monique hadn't rescued me in this very parking lot, all those weeks ago, I don't think I would even be standing here. So now it's time for you to take some of your own advice, right Monique?" She shoots me a glance and I wholeheartedly agree.

"Well ladies, I don't really know what to say for once. I'm usually so organized and planned out, and now here I am just winging it, day by day." Her tone is full of disappointment, deflated.

Stephanie chuckles as she points out, "luckily for you Char, I've been winging it since the day I was born, and I can teach you how to fly by the seat of your pants too." We all laugh out loud, happy to have made it past the tension.

We notice the youngest kids making their way out the door, and recognize our cue to fetch our kiddies. From the back seat, I wrap my arms around Charlotte's shoulders, as Stephanie lays a hand on her forearm. "You are not alone," I reassure her, "Stephanie and I are with you every step of the way." She nods her agreement to us, and we exit the car.

"We'll send the kids out to you," Stephanie promises, and we give our friend a wave. As we re-enter the building, Steph whispers to me, "So, I guess that's the end of the brandy coffees then." She remarks with a raised eyebrow.

"Oh Stephanie, you truly are awful." I swat at her, as we head off to grab the kids.

Stephanie

5th Thursday

As I sit in the waiting room, I realize a lot has changed in recent weeks. This office is the same, but the woman sitting here has changed more than I could have imagined. I feel 10 years younger. I feel… happy! I didn't realize how truly unhappy I was until Nate left. I thought my world had ended, when in fact, I just hadn't been living; I was simply existing in a role I no longer enjoyed but felt trapped in.

Even with my recent date disasters, I feel happier now than I have in years. Liam and Lucy seem more settled. Sure, it's a change for them to have to go to see their dad at Grandma's, but from what they've shared, he actually spends time with them now. He even brought them to lunch and played a game with them. I can't remember the last time he had ever done any of those things when we were still together. He left all the parenting to me, in fact, he had little to no relationship with his children.

The receptionist smiles over at me, "Catherine will see you now." She motions with her head for me to go straight through the doors. I smile my thanks as I pass her desk, and spot Catherine waiting for me in her doorway at the end of the hall.

"Have a seat Steph, we've got a lot to get through." I sit in the leather studded chair opposite her desk, and eye the piles of paperwork around us. Was this all pertaining to my case? "I've heard back from Mr. Gamble, Nate's lawyer, and I'm hoping by tweaking our final proposal, we can get an agreement and avoid court proceedings." She smiles at me reassuringly, but I'm not convinced. I just can't see Nate giving in to all our terms.

"How much tweaking are we talking?" If I don't get full spousal support, there's no way the kids and I can stay in our home. I feel my nails digging into my palms, already anxious.

"I think we need to change our strategy a little. For you, this case is about securing a future for you and the kids, but for Nate, I think this case is more about his ego and we need to play to that." Catherine informs me with a slow mischievous smile. I raise my left brow in confusion. "Nate is showboating his parenting. His lawyer has included in-depth details about his visits with the kids to demonstrate what a brilliant father he can be with them. He

142

can't play the 'amazing dad' routine and wish to cut off their financial support, so I think we should play up to that. His lawyer is attempting to show that you stood in Nate's way from developing this amazing relationship with his kids. I intend to request for your spousal support to remain at the same amount, but to increase visitations. Currently, we have agreed that Nate can have the children every other weekend and alternate holidays. I wish to add Wednesday after school, until 8pm, as an extra visitation." She holds up a hand to pause my interruption. I was clear that I do not want to give Nate more time with the kids. "Nate's pride will see this as a huge win, when in fact, we both know after a while he will be too busy for this arrangement and then he'll have to ask you to keep the kids on those nights. Trust me, I've dealt with slime balls like Nate many times, I think this is our best advantage."

I look at her uncertainly. I know she thinks this play on pride will suck Nate in, but I'm skeptical. "What if he accepts the Wednesday visitation but still refuses the spousal support amount? Then I'll have lost even more." I confide my underlying fears.

Catherine shakes her head. "It doesn't work like that. I've made it clear this is our last and final negotiation. I have us registered for court in two weeks, so if Mr. Gamble does not encourage Nate to accept this deal, then all bets are off and we start anew with the judge." She explains, matter-of-factly. "Steph, I've spoken off the record with Clive Gamble and it seems like Nate's primary focus is to have a permanent agreement as soon as possible. Until he has a separation agreement signed by a judge, he's unable to make any financial decisions. Basically, the longer this plays out, the longer he's stuck at his Mom's, and his lawyer inferred that has not been working out too well. I think this is our trick card and we should play it now, but I need you to be 100% sure of this. What do you say?" She tilts her head at me, and her face is filled with a bright white smile.

I have never noticed how beautiful Catherine is before. Her severe demeanour detracts from her facial features. Her little button nose and plump cheeks are perfectly paired with her twinkling eyes. When she's excited, the corners of her mouth lift up, just a touch. A suggestion of playfulness in complete confliction with her serious persona. She's like an onion. The outside is just wrapping, protecting the inside until each layer is peeled back to reveal the beauty within. There was way more to Catherine than anyone could guess. I think she likes it that way. Her austerity has been purposely developed to keep people away, and only the patient, interested people get to see the real deal. "I'm in, Catherine. I trust you, and I know you're the best in the business." I nod my agreement, and I'm rewarded with the light that floods her face from her beaming smile. "I hope it's not inappropriate, but if I had a smile like that, that lit up my face, I would smile all day every day, Catherine."

Sadness flickers across her face and I realize I've hurt her feelings. Me and my big friggen mouth! God, Steph, you need to learn when to shut up! "I'm sorry, I didn't mean to make you feel uncomfortable."

She interrupts my stammering, "No Steph, honestly you're fine. It's me, I'm sorry. Stanton said almost the exact same thing to me last night. I've been so busy and career focused lately that I guess I've 'lost' my smile. I seem to have forgotten what makes me happy, and the realization of that has made me sad. Life never turns out as we expect, but I've been luckier than most, and I hadn't realized I was dwelling on the missing, instead of concentrating on what I already have."

I was in shock. Perfect, tough, controlled Catherine has doubts and insecurities just like the rest of us. "I mean, most of us are in awe of you Catherine, I can't even imagine any area in life where you do not excel. I guess this really is proof that we aren't always as we seem, right?" I reach across the desk and grab her warm hand. The gesture is unfamiliar to her and she instinctively pulls her hand back, embarrassed.

"Sorry, I'm not used to people touching me." Her cheeks flush, and I can see she's embarrassed to have opened up to me. I decide to tell her how I met Monique and Char.

Tears of laughter stream down her face as I finish recounting my dreadful wailing and Char tapping on the car window, refusing to leave. "Wow, thanks Steph, I needed that." She wipes her face with a tissue from the mahogany box on the corner of her desk, and her shoulders relax. She's laughed the uptightness away.

"You've been amazing to me, Catherine. I'm not even the same woman that walked into this office only weeks ago, and I have you to thank for that. So, whatever shortcomings you're dwelling on, forget about them. You have an enormous impact on other people's lives, and even mental wellbeing. Don't ever forget that. Maybe you spend too much time in your work? Listen, tonight why don't you join us at our table for a change? Leave your work at home and just come over for a laugh and a chat." I can see her hesitation and I rise from my seat, gathering my bag and coat. "I don't want to take up any more of your professional time, but I've had a great time chatting with you, so we'll continue tonight." I smile at her and wave, before she can continue in her protest.

I'm the first at our table tonight. Feeling determined to catch Catherine when she arrives, before she sets up her makeshift office. I spy Lexi skip to the front of the girl's group and only seconds later, Catherine appears, scouring the room for a quiet spot to set up. I wave my hand to get her attention, but she is purposefully looking the opposite way. I suspect she is hellbent on pretending she can't see me.

My chair makes a shrill scrape as I push it back and head towards her. "Catherine, I'm over here. I've saved you a seat."

She sighs as she turns to me, "Steph, I know you mean well but honestly, I have a ton of work to complete." She shrugs like it's not her decision.

"That's awesome." I say, as I lead her by the elbow. "The great thing about work is that it will be there tomorrow." I smirk as we reach our table at the back of the room.

"Evening girls." Monique has joined us, and is smiling, looking from me to Catherine, amused by our tussle. "Don't bother trying to get your laptop out here, Stephanie and Charlotte are relentless once they have an idea in their mind."

I'm not relentless, or at least I don't think I am. Oh God, maybe I am. Charlotte must be rubbing off on me. I've dragged this poor woman halfway across the room, and as the red flush of her neck rise to her cheeks, I feel guilty for interfering. "Hey

147

Steph, Monique, oh, and I'm gonna presume you're Catherine. Hi, I'm Charlotte." She gives her a half wave as she settles in her seat.

"Hi Charlotte, great to meet you." Lucky for me, Catherine's good manners are forcing her into conversation.

"Catherine, it's nice to finally meet you, we've heard such great things about you from Steph. I'm so glad you've joined us." Char's genuine tone and warmth are like an enveloping hug, and I'm thankful to her for helping put Catherine at ease. Spotting the coffees on the table, I cast a sideways glance at Monique. Clearly, I wasn't discreet enough, as Char interrupts me, "Listen ladies, I'm still gonna bring coffee. Today I brought a flask for you all so you wouldn't miss it tonight, but from now on, I'll bring the coffees and one of you bring the flask, ok?" She looks around at us open and unashamed.

"Stanton has a lovely, aged brandy in his den at home. I'm sure he'll never miss me swiping a few shots from it, so as a newcomer, I would love to contribute if that's ok?" Catherine fills the silence without realizing that she has helped us all avoid a potentially awkward moment.

I raise my cardboard coffee cup towards her, "I knew you'd fit right in." Monique and Char also lift their cups, as Catherine's cheeks blush. I look around at the four of us. A misfit of women with nothing in common, yet here we are, united together.

Gabrielle

6th Tuesday

I am tidying the front desk when the studio phone rings. "Hello, Gabrielle speaking, how may I help you?"

"Gabby? Thank goodness. It's Christopher, listen, I'm running late, and I was just wondering if you could take my 11:30 bootcamp session?" His voice sounds breathless, and for a second, I think I hear another voice giggling.

Come on Gabrielle, this is your chance to stand up for yourself. I will myself to speak up, "Actually, Chris, I have an appointment already booked for today. I would be more than happy to take on a few more classes if you want us to sit down and review the schedule sometime?" I am trying my very best to keep my voice level. He intentionally called me Gabby. He knows I prefer Gabrielle, but uses the diminutive Gabby whenever he wants to make me feel less than, and I am done accepting these passive aggressive little moves. I never call him Chris, and I am sure this has not gone unnoticed.

"Hmmm, you're right. Maybe we should review your teaching schedule soon. If your availability is not as flexible as before, then I certainly need to take that into account." I am dumbfounded as his words echo down the line. I am positive I hear another voice in the background, I'm sure of it.

Take a deep breath, inhale and count to three, I urge myself. Channeling an inner calm, I don't actually feel. "My availability has always remained flexible and my commitment to the studio has always been 100%. I'm disappointed you would insinuate otherwise. Honestly, I don't think it's fair or professional for you to make remarks in this manner, hoping to guilt me into taking your class, Christopher." There, I've said it! I hold my breath, proud of myself for calling him out, but also nervous of the backlash I fear will ensue.

Down the line, I hear an intake of breath and a murmured 'how dare she'. Omg, he actually has me on loud speaker while his boyfriend Stephen is listening in the background. The giggling I thought I heard at the beginning of the call made sense now. "I had no idea you were so unhappy, Gabrielle. Clearly we need to sit down and define some boundaries." I am surprised by his immediate understanding, despite the cold tone of his voice. "I need people I can rely on, who don't throw their dummy out of the pram anytime they can't have things their own way."

Am I insane? Is he honestly trying to turn this on me? For years I've supported him and his studio at the cost of my own financial wellbeing. I often put my family on a back burner to help out extra, or cover unpaid shifts, and now Christopher was going to have the audacity to belittle and berate me? No. I will not stand for it. Enough is enough. "Actually, a client has just come in, so we will have to finish this chat next time I see you. I hope you manage to resolve your class for today. Bye." I hang up. Without taking a breath, without allowing a pause for Christopher to jump in with his retorts. A calm washes over me as though I am in a trance, and for the first time in a long time, I know exactly what I need to do. I head to the large studio at the back, grab my bag and switch off the lights. I pass through the kitchen and collect my mug, water bottle and bag of healthy protein snacks.

I slam the front entrance door behind me and engage the double barrel lock. "Goodbye Studio, Goodbye Christopher!" I walk towards my car without a backward glance, and drive home on auto-pilot.

༄ঌ

Lola is waiting at the door to greet me. Her fluffy tail wagging so fast, her little bum is shaking from side to side. She really is the cutest pup ever. "Awhhh, my little Lolita. Always here to make mommy feel better, isn't that right?" She runs little circles around me, so excited to have me home. Rushing into the front living room, she barks at the couch. She wants me to sit and groom her. Her cuteness pulls at my heartstrings. I have nothing better to do, so I flop down into the couch. I reach into the side table drawer for Lola's brush and comb as she jumps up eagerly beside me. As I smooth and tame her fluffy hair, I tell her all about my morning and her big wide eyes look back at me. She licks my forearm and nestles close into my chest. Comforting me.

It's completely ridiculous to think my dog can understand me, but just talking out loud allows me to let the stress of the morning float away. Suddenly I realize I'm relieved. No more walking on eggshells, no more over eager, happy to help Gabrielle. The strain of always being willing and able has taken its toll on me, and I have been feeling weighed down with all the pressure. I feel proud of myself, and in this moment, I know I am never going back to teach at the studio again. I don't know what I will do, but

152

at least I know what I won't be doing. The knowledge of knowing I made the right decision, combined with the calmness of the house and Lola's gentle breathing against my chest, lull me into a content, relaxed sleep.

တ<del></del>တ

I feel Lola jump off me, and hear her nails clickety click on the hard wood floor as she runs to the front door. I urge myself to ignore the sound of a key in the lock so I can to stay in this gorgeous slumber. I hear steps approach and stop. I rouse myself enough to open my eyes and see Max's face filled with concern. "Hey honey, how was your day?" I ask. My voice sounds croaky, still filled with sleep.

"Better than yours, I'm guessing? What's going on, are you unwell Gabrielle? Why didn't you call me, I could have grabbed you something from the pharmacy?" He sits on the edge of the couch and checks my forehead with the palm of his hand, feeling for a temperature.

I sit up slightly and smile. "No Max, I'm not sick, in fact, I feel fantastic." I am surprised to discover this is completely true. I feel great, I feel light, I feel hopeful. I hadn't realized that I had lost these feelings recently. Allowing myself to be taken for granted had chiselled away at my optimistic attitude, and I had been feeling drained and weighed down. "For the first time in a while, I feel great, Max. I've left the studio and Christopher. I have no intention of ever going back."

I look deep into Max's eyes so he can see how determined I am. His big strong arms reach around me and he pulls me close into a bear hug. "This is the best news I could hope for." He whispers into my hair. I realize how much Max and the kids have had to put up with. How many sacrifices I made but essentially, they were their sacrifices. Missing out on family fun because I just needed to finish some admin for the studio. Giving up our Saturday and Sunday brunches because Christopher wanted his weekend mornings to be with Stephen, so I had to cover the weekend classes. I feel like a fool who couldn't see. I had been on the hamster wheel unable to recognize that I wasn't actually getting anywhere. Just putting in a lot of hard work for little to no return.

I hold onto Max's strong embrace; thankful he'll support me and whatever the future holds. "How come you're home anyways?" I lay my head against his chest as he leans further back into the couch.

"We were short some capping for Mrs. Reynold's roof and I thought I might have a pack in the garage, saving me a trip to the yard," he explains, and I smile. Max is an amazing and hard worker, but there is rarely a job where he isn't short something or other. He is a true optimist. If he thinks the job will cost the customer $2500 in materials, then that's what he'll charge. At the end of the job when the actual material costs more like $2750, he never charges that back to the customer. When he gauges a job will take 3 days, but it's more like four and a half, he takes that loss on the overall profit of the job. He never loses money, but he's often paying himself less than his workers with all the unpaid hours he puts in. I constantly tell him to increase his prices and factor in for unexpected costs, but he always reminds me that his customer service is why he has never been out of work in 18 years and constantly has jobs lined up. It's true. Max has given all of himself to those years, but it has built him a solid reputation in town, and people appreciate him. I had been doing the same thing, but not reaping any of the benefits. I often thought Max foolish for 'wasting' his time, but here I was, the biggest fool of them all.

I sighed, trying to release the guilt and frustration that was building inside of me. "Hey, no overthinking this Gabrielle, ok? You've put this decision off way longer than Christopher ever deserved, but what's done is done now. No over analyzing or feeling bad over how things got to this point, right? You're out of there, and the future is bright, and that's it, ok?" He lifts my chin with his forefinger to meet his gaze, and I nod with a sheepish smile. He knows me too well and I am grateful for that. He lifts himself off the couch and holds out his hand towards me.

"Are you going back to work now?" I sink back into the couch lazily.

Max shakes his head and gives my hand a tug. "No, I'm gonna take my lunch break now. Why don't you run upstairs? I'll grab a candle and we can see if we can work together to help you release a little more of that tension, how does that sound?" His left eyebrow lifts as he gives me a cheeky grin. I pull his hand back with full force, until he topples onto me on the couch.

"I don't think I can wait that long..." He cuts me off as his mouth covers mine, and the stress and worries of the day melt away.

∽∾

"Mom, I'm so excited you're free tonight to watch our rehearsal." Karla is grinning from ear to ear. The girls were delighted when they found out I had left my job at the studio. I thought they loved having a dynamic working mom, but I was wrong. They just want a happy, available mom, and I am determined to be that for them. I turn in my seat and smile back at Karla as I detach my seatbelt.

"Well, I can't wait to see what you can do." I ruffle her hair as she steps out of the backseat, and we head together into the hall.

The girls rush over to their friends and I scan the room to see if any of the other moms I know have arrived. I notice Monique at the back table talking with Steph and head over to join them. "Well, if anyone is strong enough, it's Charlotte. She's got this." I catch the end of Monique's sentence, as Steph is nodding in agreement.

I clear my throat a little to announce my presence. I don't want them to think I was eavesdropping, but now I'm concerned. "Hi ladies, I'm sorry, I couldn't help but overhear. Has something happened with Charlotte?" I catch them exchanging glances, unsure if they should divulge what they were talking about. "Girls, I have been friends with Charlotte for years. I can't believe something has happened and I am unaware. I mean, I just saw you all last week at yoga." Steph looks around furtively, ensuring no one else is around, and gives me a quick resume of the past week and Charlotte's recent struggles.

Tears sting my eyes. My good friend, who has supported and cheered me so many times over the years, has been struggling and I was completely unaware. She clearly didn't feel she could reach out to me. I'm truly a bad friend. "Oh Gabrielle, don't be upset. None of us could have foreseen this. Charlotte is normally the organised one, always in control. She didn't want us to see her vulnerable." Monique patted my shoulder reassuringly.

I nod to both of these lovely women with a forced smile. They don't know Char like I do. They weren't there in the early years when Adam would come home and she would be passed out on the couch. I was there though, and I should not have forgotten that a support system is vital to Charlotte. I had been too busy recently. How had I forgotten to check in with her, with Adam? Poor Adam, why didn't he call me?

I see her making her way across the hall, accompanied by another Mom, and I vow not to let my support slip again. "Gabrielle, it's so nice to see you." Char bends down and gives me a warm hug. I latch onto her tight and squeeze her hard. Silently willing her to know how sorry I am that I haven't been there for her, and reassuring her I'm here now, all in the same moment. "How come you're free, no class tonight?" Her eyes look a little glassy. She's holding back tears, trying to keep a brave face. I know that's important to her and I accept she doesn't want to talk about herself right now. "Have you met Catherine? Catherine, this is my friend Gabrielle." I smile at Catherine and she nods back. I can tell she's aware of the unspoken exchange between Charlotte and I; clearly, she's an intuitive woman.

With a small nod to Charlotte that it will all be fine, that we will work through this, I commence a recount of my day to the table. I give a press release version, as I know our town is small and I don't want to embarrass anyone who may be friendly with Christopher. "I only went to the Studio once before your Yoga session," Steph remarks "the guy running the class was more interested in checking himself out in the mirror and making over-the-top gay references that I really couldn't focus on enjoying the class." I burst out laughing as this perfectly summed up Christopher, and for once I didn't feel the need to defend him. I could just laugh along with the rest of the group. I expand a little more on how difficult things had become at work, and the girls are thrilled at my bravado. "It's so hard to walk away and start over, I should know! Congratulations, Gabrielle, I'm super proud of you." Steph announces, and the women around the table eagerly agree. I could instantly see why Charlotte cherished these new friendships.

"I know this isn't the time or place, and you don't know me, but it sounds to me like Christopher has broken quite a few employment guidelines. If you need someone to help draft your resignation letter and ensure you get your full notice pay, and any holidays owed to you, I would genuinely like to help you. If you'll accept." Wow, this Catherine woman was even more intuitive than I thought.

I didn't really know what to say, but I was dreading having to hash out details with Christopher, and could already imagine the gossip and slanderous remarks he will try to spread about me in the community. This could be an ideal solution to put an end to anything before it even begins. "Catherine, I would welcome that help please, but I insist on paying you."

Catherine smiles back at me, and her eyes twinkle as she says "Well why don't we incorporate solicitors' fees into your resignation letter and The Studio can pay me, how does that sound?"

I get out of my seat and hug her hard "That sounds wonderful, thank you so much."

"Oh, honestly it's nothing." Her smile has somewhat faded and she looks uncomfortable.

I glance around the table, and the others are smirking. I raise my eyebrow questioningly, urging them to let me in on the secret. "Gabrielle, Catherine hates to be touched, which kind of sucks for her cause we're all huggers in this group." Steph explains and they all burst out laughing, even Catherine. The redness from her cheeks fade, as her eyes dance with laughter.

Charlotte

6th Thursday

Two more minutes and I'm done. I mop the sweat that has beaded on my forehead and focus on my breathing. I drink from my water bottle greedily; thankful I've completed another session. I've been walking 3 miles a day on our treadmill, and I'm really feeling the benefits. The adrenaline courses through my veins and I feel invigorated. Dr. Kelsey recommended I try to find some healthy habits to aid with my anxiety, and after much research through mental health forums, I started with walking.

I could never have imagined the simple idea of walking daily would improve my mood so much, but it has. I feel proud of my achievement, and infused with energy for the day. My body now craves healthier options, as if it knows I'm trying to re-start it.

No doubt the pills are also helping tremendously. Unlike previous medications, I can still feel, and am very invested in everyday interactions. I am not dulled down or fazed out; the over thinking and paranoia have definitely calmed down though. I'm not second guessing my every thought and action. Or looking for hidden meanings behind Adam's words. At last, I am learning to accept things as they're said, and not as I interpret to hear them. I've only had one session with my new therapist, Brenda, but I am already working hard on the recommendations she's made for me.

The moment I met Brenda; I knew I would be well again; I would make it through this. As I explained how badly things had deteriorated and what brought me to seek help, she simply nodded and made notes. When I finished my explanations and justifications, she laid down her pencil and smiled at me. "Charlotte, you have been juggling so many emotions and responsibilities for so long. You should feel proud of yourself for knowing you need a little extra help." I was astounded. This wasn't what I had been expecting at all. No admonishments? No disapproving tones? No raking over all my failures? That first session in therapy had taught me I didn't need anyone to judge me, as I had been doing that to myself my whole life, and finally it was time to give myself a break. I left her office feeling so light. Like when you were a kid, and you went ice skating. Your skates would hurt for the first while until you warmed up, but then you would get used to them. Once you took them off, though, your feet felt weightless. That's how I felt when I left her office. Weightless. Free.

Since that day, I've been working hard at being honest with myself, and recognising what is real and what is 'my idea' of a situation. The medication allows me to look at my actions objectively; it's giving me room to breathe. For the first time in years, I no longer feel as though I'm constantly holding my breath. I push the stop button on the treadmill, gather my towel and water bottle, and head upstairs to shower.

The heat hits my skin and I can feel my muscles being soothed with the pulsating jets. I turn off the overhead rain-shower head and lather my hair. The rest of the side jets remain on. Adam had this Shower Spa installed for us 5 years ago, and I don't think I used it as anything but a basic shower. Normally I would take a four-minute quick shower as to not waste water or my time. I would plan dinner during that time, or make a list of chores I still needed to complete. It would seem ridiculous for me to spend twenty minutes just enjoying and relaxing in the shower.

Now, I was learning to relax. I was learning to appreciate living in the moment, and not having to plan or prepare for the next catastrophe coming my way. I had been so unaware that I was living like that. I thought I was happy, but my intent to control everyone and everything around me had weighed me down until I could no longer let go.

I was grateful now for what I term as my 'breakdown'. In fact, it had been a 'breakthrough'! I was no longer fretting over tomorrow and the 'what if's'. Finally, learning to live for today. It wasn't easy and I know I will be working on this for weeks, months, even years to come, but I feel so darn hopeful for myself.

Adam has been amazing, as always. Levi is a little sceptical; it will take some time for me to earn back his trust 100%, but that's ok, he has the right to move at his own pace. Grace knows that I've been feeling unwell and need a little extra help to feel better. I see her side glances, worrying if I'm ok, and I am doing my best to reassure her. No longer apologizing for being fallible. I'm accepting myself for who I am and hoping those around me can do the same.

As I finish dressing, the doorbell rings. I pop my wet hair in a messy bun and make my way down the stairs. Through the sunlit glass door, I can make out a female silhouette. "Gabrielle, to what do I owe this surprise?" I open the door wide and motion her in. As I close the door, she reaches and hugs me.

"Char, I'm sorry. I've been wrapped up in my own troubles and I didn't see that you were struggling. I wish I could have been there for you and Adam. Are you ok? Are you coping? What can I do?" Her worried face looks at me so intently that I chuckle.

I take her hand and lead us into the front room. "Honestly Gabrielle, I'm doing great, and it's not your responsibility to worry about me. You've done that for our whole fifteen-year friendship and I should never have allowed it. I should never have taken such advantage. It's a two-way street. I should have reached out to you. I mean, you left the studio and I didn't even know you were struggling. It's me who should be apologizing." I smile and pat her hand, reassuring her my words are sincere.

She releases a long breath, "The last thing I wanted was to add more drama to your plate." She admits.

"Well, I've thrown a lot of drama at you over the years, so I think I owe you a few." I wink at her to show her I'm joking. In this instant, I am beyond grateful for my friendship with Gabrielle. Over the years, we have grown like sisters. We know each other too well. I know her mannerisms and attitudes. She knows my weaknesses and struggles. We have different personalities and can totally rub each other the wrong way, annoying the other one, but ultimately, we hold one another up.

Gabrielle and I spend the afternoon catching up on recent events in one another's lives, that have led us to this point. Both of us having reached impasses in our lives, and carving out new paths. Instead of commiserating on the difficulties of the past, we are fuelled with hope for the future and what may lay ahead. "I'm glad you showed up today, Gabrielle. We needed this." I smile at her as she gathers her things, eager to get home before the school bus drops the girls home.

She hugs me tightly, "You're doing great, Char. I'm so proud of you." She rubs my arm up and down, as though warming me. She's always been very tactile, but the more she worries about me, the more arm rubbing she does. To this day, I don't know if it's cultural or just simply Gabrielle, but I love it. I give her a big kiss and wave her goodbye. As I close the door, a sense of peace washes over me. Over the years, we've met men, chosen husbands, had babies, and dealt with all the ups and downs of life, but ultimately, we made it through. We would both be just fine. Deep down inside, I knew it.

৩৯৫৩

As I approach our usual table, I smile to see Gabrielle already installed, chatting happily with our new friends. When I first met Steph and Monique, I worried Gabrielle would feel left out, but I could see she was as enchanted with these women as I was. Catherine was also seated with us; I was delighted Steph had strong armed her into our group. I am sure we are a different breed to what she's normally used to, but I hope she's enjoying our company and being out of her comfort zone.

"Ladies, good evening." I smile around at each of them and they greet me warmly.

Steph pats the chair next to her. "Sit here Char, I've been waiting for you to get here to fill you all in on my disastrous date." I take the seat eagerly, knowing Steph's story will be a roller coaster ride. She looks around the table to ensure she's got our full attention.

"First, I just want to pre-empt this by saying, this whole scenario was completely out of character for me, ok?" We all nod in agreement, encouraging her to continue. Monique catches my eye and we both try hard to not already begin laughing.

"So, I was working a training shift yesterday during lunch, and I was serving a group of businessmen. They were busy discussing long and short options, which I had no idea what any of that meant, so I did my best to be as little disturbance to them as possible. I took their orders, brought them drinks, served their meals and then brought the check. All was well, but as they were leaving, one man beckoned me over to the table. By the time I made my way there, he was the only person remaining. I ask him if everything is ok, and he says, 'correct me if I'm wrong but aren't you Stephanie Firth?' As he's asking, I recognise him from somewhere. Then it clicks. It's Brad, this guy I went to high school with. We hung out in the same friend group, but never dated or anything, and after high school we kind of just lost touch. Anyways, he asked me if I'd like to join him for dinner that evening and the kids were going to Nate's, so I thought why not and said yes."

Every single one of us is hunched forward at the table, listening intently to Steph's whispered account. The fact that for once our table was so quiet was probably drawing attention to us, but we were oblivious as we cheered Steph on with her story. "I give him my address and he say's he'll pick me up at eight. As the time approaches, I start to feel nervous and kinda regret agreeing to the date, but I know it's too late to back out now. The doorbell rings, I open the door and he's standing there wearing a full suit and holding out a bottle of merlot. I feel completely underdressed in my black ripped jeans and blouse, and ask him if I should change. He reassures me we're just going to a local sports bar and not to worry. Says our table is for nine so why don't we open the bottle and have a pre dinner drink? I'm feeling so nervous and could do with a glass of Dutch courage, so I agree and usher him inside to the kitchen. We talk awkwardly for ten minutes about people from school who we've lost contact with or who we've recently seen, and slowly I can feel the wine starting to relax me. We chat easily and make our way to the bar. We arrive at the Loose Moose," poor Steph has to pause at this point because the rest of us have started laughing uncontrollably. "I kid you not. We enter, and he informs the host he's reserved a table, but we wish to sit in the bar side. Ok, I defo thought this was strange, like we're on a date, he's overdressed and now wants to sit in the bar, like not a nice cozy booth? Anyways, the hostess sits us and a barmaid comes over and takes our drink order. I order a glass of wine, not wishing to mix my drinks, and he orders a white Russian. Once our drink orders are taken, he reaches across the table, takes my hand, and says, 'you know Steph, in high school, all the guys in our group wanted to date you but you only had eyes for Nate. It was so annoying and obviously didn't work out'. Like I wanted to be flattered, but I was becoming annoyed.

Our drinks arrived and I chugged half my wine, hoping it would help me be less irritable, when our waitress arrived at the table. 'Hey Steph, long time no see', she says to me. At that point, I realize our server is Amy Green, also from our high school. 'Back again so soon, Brad?', she says, as she smiles coyly at him. Ok a little back story here, Amy was a year ahead of us at school, head cheerleader, prom queen, you get the picture. Brad had been completely infatuated with her and she didn't even know he existed. Now here I was at the table, and the two of them had forgotten my existence as they spent the next ten minutes chatting and reminiscing, while I stood there drinking my wine like a spare part." She raises her eyes and looks pointedly at Monique as she picks up her coffee cup.

"Then, I receive a text from Steph saying, **Help, date fail, please call me and pretend there's an emergency**." Monique fills us in. "I dial her number and ask if she's safe, does she need a ride? Like what can I do? Then I hear Steph answer me, 'Chlamydia? Oh! The tests are positive? Ok well I guess I better get to the pharmacy right away'. And she hangs up as I'm howling down the other end of the phone." We all join in Monique's laughter and face back to Steph, hungry for more details.

"So, needless to say, Brad and Amy are both looking at me as I hang up and I say, 'I think I better go, I've got some things to deal with'. Amy, bless her, looks super embarrassed and says she'll give us a few minutes to ourselves. Brad then looks at me and says 'listen Steph, I'm sure you feel very awkward right now, but trust me, this can happen to anyone. We can just fool around, no full-on penetration to be safe, ok?'

"No, please tell me he did not say that." Catherine is clearly horrified at the unravelling of this story. Her shock and disgust simply increase the hilarity of the situation to the rest of us.

"Oh, he said precisely that! Right then I remembered why our group had lost touch with Brad. He had been dating three girls in our group simultaneously without the others knowing. His nickname was Brad the Cad! I don't know how I forgot that. I told him I didn't think things were gonna work out, and I ordered an uber. He tried to change my mind, but once he saw my mind was made up and it was futile, he told me he only invited me out to make Amy jealous, and had just been using me anyways. He said he wished me luck and hoped I might find someone as kind as him, willing to over look my infectious disease! Can you imagine?" She looks at each one of us, shaking our heads and commiserating with her at how truly awful her date was.

"She hasn't even told you the best bit yet." Monique looks challengingly at Steph, who shakes her head. "Ok I will tell them for you. On her way home, Stephanie is feeling a bit sorry for herself and she facetimes me and starts crying. I reassure her that Brad is just a dick, and then she receives a text from him telling her if it doesn't work out with Amy, and her condition clears up, he'll be wiling to give her a second chance." Spasms are literally overtaking Monique as tears of laughter flow down her face. I am acutely aware of Steph's embarrassment, and the redness on her face is now a glowing beacon around our table.

"I mean, it could have been worse." Steph announces. We look at her doubtfully. "I could have let him discover my flappy bird."

At this point, we are stunned into silence. No one seems sure what to say or do next. "uhm... what's a flappy bird?"

The Unicorn Moms

Gabrielle asks, and our table dissolves into riotous laughter to the hushing and shushing from the other moms nearby.

Catherine

7th Tuesday

"Catherine, I have Mr. Gamble on the line for you."

"Perfect, Jane, buzz him through, thanks." I see the red flashing light beside line one, as the receptionist transfers the call. I wait almost a full minute before picking up the line. I anticipated his call, but not so soon. This was a good sign for me. Clearly, he wants to negotiate.

"Hi Clive, sorry to keep you, but I have a very full agenda today. Is there something I can help you with?" I love playing it coy with some of these older fuddy-duddy types. As if I wasn't fully aware that my recent proposal to them was worded in such a fashion to elicit panic.

"Thanks for taking my call, Catherine. I've received your proposal regarding the Lynch separation agreement, and I want to clarify a few issues with you."

I bet you do, I silently taunt. "Oh, were any of my points unclear?" I request in my most innocent voice.

I could hear pages turning in the background. "In your summation, you have alluded that should my client not accept your present proposal, you and your client will no longer be willing to settle this separation amicably. You further mention the irreparable damage that will be made to my client's reputation, when the subject of adultery is exposed in court, and I just wanted to clarify exactly what threats you seem to be making towards my client." His voice was stern, as though he was chastising a young child.

I left his words to hang in silence for a moment, knowing my calm unphased reaction would panic him further. "Listen, Clive, we both know that this is Nate's last opportunity to settle out of court. Stephanie Lynch has irrefutable evidence regarding her husband's affair. She currently hopes to avoid court proceedings, as she wishes to focus on the wellbeing of her children. However, she is adamant that should she be forced to take the embarrassing route to court, she will use all evidence in her possession to fully expose your client's actions to the judge. You and I both know that no Judge will look favourably on Nate's actions. During his first visit with his children at his mother's house, only 6 days after leaving my client, he introduced Levi and Lucy to his side piece. How do you think the judge will react to little Lucy sharing that information with us all?" I can hear Clive sputtering down the line, intent on objecting, but I'm done playing games, so I cut him off. "I have a client waiting in the conference room. You have until the end of tomorrow's business day to get your client to agree to our terms, or I will file papers with the court first thing Monday. We are past the point of negotiation now. Have a great afternoon." I drop the phone back in its cradle as a victorious smile reaches my lips. Clive knows he has lost. I know he has lost. I am confident that by tomorrow afternoon, I will have a signed agreement sitting on my desk. It's the least Stephanie deserves.

స్త్రీ

My phone chimes as I push open the front door. My doorbell app is letting me know someone's at the door. I love the security of it, but it also annoys me when I'm the one coming home. A true example of how women are never happy, I guess!

175

I make my way to the bedroom to hang up my blazer and change into some more relaxed clothes. I find a nice pair of stretch jeggings and pull them on. They're stiff as I try to pull them over my stomach. I really need to make a plan and commit to losing this extra weight. Lexi is going to be eight this year. The excuses need to stop. Initially, I didn't care about getting my figure back; I was just enthralled being a mom. As the months turned to a year and we explored IVF treatments again for a second child, I knew the extra weight increase was a side effect of the treatments, and I thought it would be a small price to pay for another baby.

Stanton and I had stopped IVF over two years ago, and resigned ourselves that Lexi would be an only child. I'm not sorry for myself, though, I know I'm one of the lucky ones. Lexi is more than enough. If I'm being honest, I didn't really acknowledge or accept that we had closed the door on that dream. Since then, we've been reluctant to make new dreams. I've been scared to be vulnerable again. I love being Lexi's mom and Stanton's wife, but I've carried the feeling of failure with me. Deep down I thought it was my fault, and I still carry that guilt with me. Some days I feel so heavy with it, that I just want to go back to work so I don't have to think; so I won't need to acknowledge my feelings.

"It has to stop." I decide, as I stare back at my reflection in the full-length mirror. Tears streak across my face and I am stunned to discover I am crying. I don't cry. I'm tough. I take care of other people who cry. There's an extra roll of skin spilling over my jeggings that I can't quite pack into my pants. I need to start working out and eating better. I need to let go of the past and its regrets, and look to the future and its possibilities. Most of all, I need to stop resenting Stanton. Keeping him at arm's length, and distancing myself so that he won't guess my disappointment and shame. Things have improved in the last few weeks. We've had a few nice evenings and been able to reconnect again, but it's still not enough. Those have been the few nights I've been with the other Mom's from theatre, and have arrived home in a fun mood after their silly stories.

"Hey, I thought I heard you come home." Stanton stands in the doorway, taking me in. I must look a mess, half dressed with mascara residue on my cheeks.

I give him a meek smile. Hoping he can read the thousand unspoken words, my heart cannot speak. "Want some help?" He approaches and gestures to the waistband on my pants. A chuckle escapes me as he grabs each side of my pants and pulls them up as I jump down.

We used to do this after Lexi's birth. He would help me literally 'jump' into my outfits. The silliness of it has me laughing, and I can see through the creases around Stanton eyes that he's happy I let him help. "It's just a few extra pounds, Catherine, nothing worth getting upset about." He whispers softly, as he strokes my cheeks with his thumbs.

I lean my head against his chest and let out a deep sigh. The softness of his shirt feels comforting. His strong arms wrap around me and he kisses the top of my head. "It's all right, I've got you." He reassures me, and a sob escapes my throat. Tears course down my face as though a dam has broken, and I cling onto Stanton as hard as I can.

He maneuvers us closer to the bed and carefully sits on the edge, pulling me down with him. "I'm sorry, I don't know what's come over me recently." I apologize.

He shakes his head, and the silver highlights in his loose curls catch the sunlight coming in the bedroom window. "It's ok to let go, to need to release all those feelings, Catherine. I feel it too sometimes. You know, we have so much, but we gave up on a dream, and I think that still hurts us underneath the facade. I don't want you to pull away from me anymore. In recent weeks, I've felt you come back and I want to do whatever I can to keep you here. That smile and your teasing has come back to life, and I just want to do whatever I can to help you, do you hear me?" His voice is gentle, encouraging and supporting. I lift my eyes to meet his gaze and nod.

"I promise, I will make the changes I need to so I can get back to being that girl. I will make a plan, Stanton, and get us all back on track as a family."

He takes me back into his arms. "You're not alone. You don't have to do it on your own, you know that right? I want to be there too. I miss us." This last sentence is barely a whisper and I hear the crack in his voice. It breaks my heart.

I wasn't doing that good of a job pretending. He knew I was struggling, and he's been trying to help support me, but I've kept him at arm's length, and it's hurt him. I hug him back fiercely; vowing things will be different. His arms caress me back and within seconds, my lips are on his and I push him back further on the bed. Desire and longing for him course through my body. I do everything within my power to try to take things easy. He senses my urgency and places a finger on my lips. "Wait, why are you in such a hurry." He teases playfully. Lifting himself from the bed, he slowly unbuttons his shirt. He removes his phone from his pant pocket and fiddles with it for a moment. As he places it down on the dresser, I hear the opening bars of 'Big Spender' playing, and he continues with his hip shaking strip tease while I dissolve into giggles. As he climbs into bed with me, I remember, this is why I fell in love with Stanton. Since the moment we met, we've been best friends; he always knows how to make things right. I close my eyes and give in to him. Finally, allowing myself to let go.

⎯ ❧ ⎯

Lexi jumps out of the car before I've even unbuckled my seat belt. She dances around outside my car door, waiting for me. "Come on Mom, I just saw Lucy go in, I want to catch her up." She rattles on my window to hurry me. I wave her on. I can see the door from here and watch as she makes her way inside.

Leaning back in my seat, I breathe in deeply and relax. This is what I've been missing. Taking time, living in the moment. After a few moments, I exit my vehicle and smile. Only weeks ago, I would have taken the opportunity to stay in the car and avoid the other moms completely, but here I was making my way into the hall willingly. Looking forward to what today's meet up will bring.

"Catherine, how's it going?" Char greets me casually, as though I've always been part of the group.

I smile at everyone and am surprised when I hear myself respond "I'm actually feeling great, thanks! For the first time in a while, I feel fantastic." I sit down and feel a blush rise to my cheeks.

Instantly, the others around the table chime in. "That's awesome, Catherine. I mean I have to say, you've come out of your shell more in the last few weeks than in all the years I've seen you around." Monique smiles encouragingly.

"I don't know what would have happened to me if I hadn't met you, so I'm just grateful you're here." Steph caught and held my gaze. The others murmured their agreement.

"Gosh, thanks everyone, I'm glad I've made such an impact on the group." I joke, and eagerly search for a new topic to change the subject to. "So, what's been happening with everyone else?"

We look at one another around the table except Monique, who is looking at her perfectly manicured nails. "Monique, are you ok?" I ask gently. As she raises her head from her nail inspection, I see tears glistening in her eyes. The others have noticed too.

Monique meets our inquisitive looks and relays her fears to us. "It's Marc. I think he's keeping something from me." I've only seen her husband at a distance once or twice over the years, so I have no trite reassurances to offer.

"Why do you think that?" Steph asks. As the recently deserted wife, I think she's the only one who could really ask the question.

"Well, he's been going out in the evening to run errands, but when I offer to join him, he refuses. Tells me to stay home and relax. Then he'll be gone way longer than his errand should take and come home without the item he went for."

"What? Monique, we only met Marc briefly, but all's he talked about was you. This sounds so strange, be more specific." Char encourages her.

"Just the other evening, after supper, he said he needed to go to the sports store as they had a sale on some jogging pants he wanted. Then, when he came home over two hours later, I asked him how he got on and he said, 'great thanks', but when I asked him what he bought, he said, 'nothing fit right', so he didn't bother to make any purchases." She raises her eyebrow at us, defying us to try and normalize this behaviour.

Steph lay her palms on the table. "Ok, that does sound like he's making up excuses, but what for? I don't want to be rude but none of us think Marc is hooking up with a side chick, right? I mean look at her." We all look at Monique. Her face shines back at us, and even with worry etched into her face, she still looks stunning. It would be hard to imagine any man thinking he could find better than Monique.

"Thank you, Stephanie, I know you mean well. No, I do not suspect an affair or another woman, at least I hope not. I am scared this may be something even worse." I catch Gabrielle's questioning face, *what's worse than an affair?* "I've also noticed some of our savings have been moved from our bank account. At first I thought Marc was just supplementing our income because I lost my job at the salon, but it's a lot more than my meagre paycheck and I don't know where it's gone." She sets her hands out on the table, defeated.

Char sits upright in her chair, "Well, there you have it, Monique. He's clearly buying you a surprise. Is it your birthday or anniversary soon?" she nods encouragingly toward Monique, willing her to make her projection true.

Monique shakes her head, stopping the look of hope on Char's face. "I want to believe that, Char, but there's something else. He's being cagey and evasive. I know there's something going on, I just don't know what it is yet."

"You have to talk to him, Monique, you can't let this worry and fester, it's not healthy for you." Gabrielle advises.

Steph nods in agreement. "Yeah, nothing can be as bad as the things we make up in our head. Call him out and get to the bottom of this before it stresses you out anymore." She urges Monique. I nod my agreement too. I keep my thoughts to myself. Too many messy divorces have taught me that lies and money going missing are often signs of drug or gambling issues. I pray this time the odds are stacked in Monique's favour, and that this is not the case for her.

As we all gather our coats and kids, each woman gives Monique a hug and words of comfort. When there's only the two of us left, I look at her and say, "I'm sorry, Monique. I hope there's a simple explanation to all this, but if there's not or if you have any questions you need answered, you text me day or night, ok?"

She leans forward and embraces me. I stand there awkwardly, wishing it wouldn't be rude to remind people I hate to be touched. "Thank you so much, Catherine. Out of all of us, I hope you are the one I never need answers from." She smiles at me, knowingly. She's right, the only reason why women need answers from me are for legalities. To know their rights. I was also hoping that Monique would not need my help, and I wished her goodnight as I follow Lexi to our car, listening to her recount of rehearsal.

Monique

7th Thursday

I massage the serum into my skin using small circular motions. So many people think it's the product you use that matters, but the application is just as important. Massaging the product into your face promotes oxygen and blood flow helping to create a brighter skin tone. It also increases collagen production; many people call this routine 'the natural facelift.'

I slip on a knitted dress and tie a chain belt around my waist. I'll pair this look with my thigh-high boots, which I know Marc loves. He texted me this morning asking if we could have lunch together. I'm convinced that he's going to confess why he's been keeping secrets, and although I'm apprehensive, at least I'll finally know what Marc's been hiding from me.

I sit back down at my vanity, ready to tackle my make up. It needs to be light. I already feel emotional and can't risk my mascara running if there are tears at lunch. I pick up my deepest rouge and run a dramatic line just under my cheekbone, all the way up the side of my eye. It totally looks weird, but as I blend it in, it highlights my cheekbones to perfection. A light wand of mascara and a crimson lip stain finish off, my fresh-faced look. The lips look a little severe, but I like the contrast and they match my tumultuous feelings.

The sound of Marc's key in the door announces his arrival and I go down to meet him. "Allo Chérie," he greets me with a warm kiss. He looks happy and more relaxed than I've seen him in recent weeks.

"You're a little earlier than I expected. Did one of your clients cancel?" It's normally a problem for Marc to take time off from the salon. Just another anomaly of things that don't add up recently.

Marc takes my hand and twirls me into his embrace. "I can do whatever I wish, I am my own man. I answer to no one." He's dramatizing his voice as though he's a bad guy in a super hero movie, and despite my concerns, I laugh at his silliness. "Come, let me lead you to your carriage." He's holding my shawl out for me. I allow him to drape it over my shoulders and I fasten the oversized pin into place, so it falls just right. My stomach grumbles and I wonder where we're eating. The butterflies in my stomach continue to flutter, and I take a deep breath to try to calm them.

Marc ushers me out the door and opens the passenger seat for me. A weird feeling passes through me, almost like excitement. Marc's behaviour is not one of a guilty man, more of an enchanted child with a secret. I don't know whether to be scared or excited, either way I just want to be done with this. I can't stand living in uncertainty.

He buckles his seat belt and turns up the radio, singing along to the 80's hits blaring out of the speakers. I guess there will be no chat on the way to lunch then. Marc reaches for my hand and smiles over at me. I raise my eyebrow back questioningly, and he pats my hand, laughing. "Patience, Monique," he mocks me over the music.

He turns the truck onto East street and my heart sinks to my stomach. Taking this route inevitably means passing The Village Spa, and my feelings are still raw. I stare out my window to avoid looking at it directly and focus on some breathing techniques to quiet my mind. Suddenly, Marc is outside my window and opening my door. I hadn't even realized the car had stopped. "Marc, what are you doing." He opens the door and holds out his arm to escort me. We are standing outside Irene's Spa, and I notice the big SOLD sign stuck on the for-sale billboard.

"It's the end of an era." I look at Marc as tears sting my eyes.

He shakes his head, "No Monique, it is not the end, it's the start of an era. Me and you, ma Chérie." He's laughing and I'm wondering if he's ok or if he's having some kind of breakdown. "Don't you understand? I bought the building for you. For you, Monique. For us!"

My body shakes and I can feel my heartbeat pounding through my chest. "Wait, what? Marc, what are you saying?" I can't dare to believe it. My own salon? Tears pour down my cheeks as I try to take in Marc's explanation.

"As soon as Irene decided to sell, I called her and we worked out a fair price for you to buy the business. It's not as much as she would have gotten if she sold to a developer, but she said she had enough money to live out the rest of her days, and would rather see you finally get the chance to build a salon for yourself. She believes in you Monique, and so do I." He pulls my hand and we walk toward the main doors.

As Marc unlocks the door, I look around, wondering if I'm dreaming. Could this be true? "Marc, how will we afford this? The Spa wasn't making very much money you know." Irene couldn't make the figures work, why would it be different for me? Doubt and fear fill my head and I look worriedly at him.

"Absolute nonsense, Chérie. Anyways you have something Irene could never have. Me! I will quit my job at the salon and join you here. Our dream Monique, finally coming true.

When we were just kids, we would dream of owning a salon one day, but we had prioritized having a nice home and focusing on the kids and their education. Those ideas had always remained dreams, but now here we were, on the precipice of our own destiny. I could barely believe it. A squeal of excitement escaped me and I wrapped my arms around Marc. "I never knew how much I wanted this, until this moment Marc, you are truly the best husband a girl could ask for."

He is even more excited than I am, and walks me from room to room, envisioning possibilities and plans. I laugh at his exuberance, "woah you're talking about a lot of changes here, Marc, and those are expensive. Do we have money to refit this place?" I wonder where we could find that kind of money.

Marc winks at me delightedly. "It's not completed yet because of course the bank still needs your approval and signature, but I got us approved for a line of credit on the house, which will cover all the refit fees and stocking a new salon. This is real Monique, this is happening." I join in his excited laughter as he picks me up and spins me around the room.

❦

After visiting the salon, we decide to pick up a bottle of champagne and some food to celebrate with the kids. We arrive home only moments after their school buses drop them off.

"Maman, Papa, why are you both home in the middle of the day?" Olivier greets us quizzically.

"Oh, I thought I heard voices. What's going on?" Juliette appears from the upstairs landing.

"Family meeting in the kitchen please," Marc announces jovially. I follow him as he tugs at my arm playfully. "Monique, you are our guest of honour, so you sit here." He leads me to the armchair by the window and points to the bar stools for the kids. "Today, I am excited to announce to you the start of 'Elle', a modern salon for the everyday woman." The kids look at us expectantly, not sure how this announcement was anything to do with us as a family.

"Your dad has bought us Irene's salon," I clarify for them.

Juliette jumps down from her stool "Ohh emmmm geeeee! Are you serious? That's amazing, I'm so happy for you guys, well for us all!" She runs towards me, hugging me tight.

"Maman, I know you will make this business an amazing success." Olivier smiles at me, proud and excited for me.

"How could she not be a success with me on her team?" Marc is now twirling around the room like a ballerina. His confidence is contagious and I too can see the dream ahead becoming our reality. I sit back in the arm chair, watching Marc spin Juliette around the kitchen island. A lot of hard work is ahead for us, but I am convinced we will make a success of our newfound venture. I dance my way to my husband and daughter, feeling silly and self conscious, but too fired up to sit back and watch them anymore without joining in.

♋♋

"Are you coming in to watch the practice, Papa?" Olivier asks Marc as we pull into the parking lot. We had just been to our favourite restaurant downtown, Spittini's, to celebrate, and Marc was dropping us off at rehearsal.

"Actually, I think I'll head over to the salon and see if Gareth is still there. No time like the present to continue with the announcements." He looks at me and I nod. He had worked at the salon for over 10 years, and despite his bravado, I knew he would be sad to leave his friends and regulars.

"Come on, let's not be late," I call to the back seat as I get out of the car. "We'll see you at pick up, will you be ok?" I ask Marc tentatively.

"I was born ok, Monique. Do not worry your beautiful head about me, ok? Go, enjoy your evening, I'll be right here when you're done." We all wave goodbye and make our way to the hall.

I can see our table at the back is already full. As I approach, I see Charlotte and Stephanie's concerned faces looking towards me. They knew I was having lunch with Marc today, and have probably been worrying since they received no news from me all day. "Good evening everyone", I smile at everyone around the table and wink at Charlotte to let her know everything is just fine. "How's everyone today? I hope you won't mind if Juju joins us today. She's come along to hangout."

"Screw this." Stephanie interrupts. "All day I've been worrying about you, and now you stroll in with the biggest smile on your face. Spill the tea, Monique. I can't take it anymore!"

I laugh as I look at the outrage on her impatient face. "Gee Stephanie, excuse me to keep you in such suspense."

"I take it Marc is not having a secret affair then?" Even Catherine is joining in on the teasing.

"Ha ha, thankfully no," I chuckle, "but he did have a big surprise for me, and it was way bigger than I could have expected." I look around at them all, dragging out the suspense. "Marc bought Irene's salon for us to set up our own spa."

"Oh, that is amazing, Monique, you and Marc running your own place! What could be more magical?" Charlotte rises from her seat and comes over to envelop me in a hug.

Steph has joined us in the three-way hug and I shoo them back to their seats as awkward looks are thrown our way from the other tables. "Thank you everyone, I know you're all delighted for me, and if I'm honest, I still can't take it all in. I have so many ideas and plans, my head is spinning.

"Well, I for one can't wait. I'm tired of the girl at my salon and have been hoping to find a new place, so this works out really well for me." Gabrielle announces to the table at large.

"Luckily Marc bought the salon and is not a secret junkie then, Gabrielle, or that would really have screwed up your plans." Stephanie answers her sarcastically, and we all start laughing.

"I super appreciate your support, Gabrielle, thank you." I reassure her as I can see she looks puzzled that the others are making fun at her expense. We chatter along excitedly, and I am overwhelmed by the love and support from these amazing women.

"Can I have everyone's full attention, please?" Michelle is addressing the room at large. "I just want to ensure that everyone knows that next Tuesday we are meeting at the theatre, and we will do a full-dress rehearsal." Most of us nod back, confirming we've read the schedule. "I am so excited to see everyone's hard work come together. Please ensure take all your belongings today as we won't be back here until next season. Have a great evening, everyone." She concludes and we gather our belongings.

"In all my years accompanying my children to lessons and after-school activities, this has been my most enjoyable thanks to you all." I announce to our group. Everyone nods and agrees. "My kids have swimming next semester, so who's up to sign their kids up at the same time?" Steph asks, and we all rush to ask what day, time and where. Laughing when we realize our children's future commitments will depend on where our Mom friends are hanging out. I think about how lucky we all are to have found each other. This motley crew of women with nothing but everything in common.

I wave good night and make my way with the kids out to Marc, waiting for us by the entrance. Time to go home, relax and truly celebrate. Just the two of us.

Stephanie

Dress Rehearsal

I finish rolling cutlery and take a few roll-ups to my recently cleared tables. It's been a slow shift; I just have two couples finishing their drinks. That's the one thing about serving, tips are great, but for tips you need people, and people tend to come in the evening. Day shifts are always up for grabs because no one wants to come in for 4 hours just to make 30 bucks in tips, and that's on a good day.

Catherine pulled a major coup and got Nate and his lawyer to agree to all our demands. Now that he has finally agreed and signed our separation agreement, I'll be able to take the odd Friday or Saturday shift and make some real money. I'm almost fully up to speed with the menu and the POS system now, so these quieter days have definitely helped me to learn the role thoroughly.

I still can't believe that Nate eventually relented and agreed to all my terms and conditions. He swore blind to me he wouldn't, but Catherine called me with the good news on Friday, and I'm still coming to terms with the knowledge that the kids and I are financially secure at last. No more asking Nate to transfer me grocery money or having to explain anything to him. With his child and spousal support arriving on the 1st of every month, I may even be able to save some of my own extra money for treats for me and the kids.

Hailey greets a customer at the door and sits him in my section. She smiles at me as she walks past. I'm grateful for the table, but a single, lone man isn't likely to make me much extra. Still, I'm here and I might as well keep busy. I approach the gentleman's table, "Hi, I'm Steph and I'll be your server today." I give him my widest smile. "Can I get you a drink from the bar or a glass of water?" I always like to offer the option of water so if the customer chooses it, they don't feel like I'm judging that they don't want to pay for a drink. It's like I'm acknowledging that I recognize they choose the water for health reasons, and not because they're a cheapskate.

"Water will be great, Steph, thanks." The man lifts his head of mousy brown curls and I can clearly see his olive-skinned face.

He's dressed in a polo shirt and jeans, casual chic. "Will you be dining alone today?" I hand him a menu.

He takes it and gestures to the empty seat opposite. "Well yes, unless you'd like to join me." His twinkly eyes seem to be challenging me.

"I'd love to, but I'm actually at work at the moment." I try to hit back playfully, except my voice ends up high pitched and squeaky at the end. The warm flush of embarrassment works its way up my neck to my cheeks. I clear my throat awkwardly, "I'll just go and get you that water." Ugh, now my voice sounds like a pubescent fourteen-year-old who's trying to convince his friends his balls have dropped. I swing by the bar and grab a tall ice water. I stand by the fan in the corner, trying to look busy, while giving my face a moment to cool down.

Picking up the water, I bring it to the table, giving myself a stern lecture to keep any chatter to a minimum. "Here you go, do you still need a few minutes to decide?" I ask, as casually as I can muster.

Mousy curls guy looks up from his menu, and I swear I can feel him look straight through me. "Well Steph, what I really want to know is what you recommend." There is something about him. It's not the hair, though the curls are super cute. And it's not his eyes, even if from here I can see they look like caramel swirls. I can't put my finger on it, but something about him makes my legs feel like they're shaking. His tone is caressing and soothing.

"Hmmmm, well I mean, you can't beat our mushroom swiss burger with hand cut fries?" I offer, hoping he's not a vegetarian. Nothing against vegetarians, but I like my men to like meat. I don't want a man who's more worried about his body than he is about mine. What is wrong with me? His caramel eyes are now just staring at me. "Or… I um… I…. could suggest something else if you wish?" I stammer.

"Oh no, the Swiss burger sounds great, but I'd sure love to know what you were just thinking? You know, your face reads like an open book. You were thinking something nice, then something unappetizing, and then something interesting. I could watch all that play out on your face. It's mesmerizing." He's amused, and I'm embarrassed again.

"Oh, I was just trying to remember if we had any specials on today," I chuckle, hoping he'll let it go at that. He nods back at me, but I can still see the glint in his eyes. "So, are the fries good with that or would you prefer a salad?" I offer.

"Fries will be perfect Steph, thanks so much." He hands me the menu and I bring his order into the kitchen.

I enter the order into our system and check on my other two tables. Both are ready for their bills, so I print them off and leave them at their tables. Neither needed our card reader, so I thank them and wish them a great afternoon. I see next week's schedule has been posted and I'm happy to see I've been assigned 3 shifts. I must be doing quite decent as Matt doesn't give shifts easily. "How's it going, Steph?" Hailey joins me at the computer. "Table 8 looks cute," she nudges me.

"Is he? Honestly I didn't notice." I look up dead pan. She bursts out laughing and I walk away before I end up joining her. "Hey Jamie, I'm just checking on my Mushroom swiss," I call over to the Chef.

He waves his spatula at me, "just about to load it up now Steph, give me 2 minutes." He smiles, and I leave the kitchen. I noticed within my first shift or two, kitchen staff do not appreciate a server for an audience, even if it's just one or two minutes. I find something to do with my time, rather than sit there watching them like a moron. My couple at table 12 are just leaving their table and wave bye to me. "Thanks again, see you soon." I call out in a friendly tone, and grab a tray to clean off their table.

I drop the dirty dishes off at the dish pit and hear the bell signalling my order is ready. "Thanks Jamie," I call, as I pick it up and swing back out the kitchen door.

"Here you are, our finest mushroom swiss with fries." I place the food in front of him.

His eyes widen at the sight of his plate, he's impressed by the size of the burger. "Now that's what I call a burger." He picks up a fry, "but are these as good as they look?" he challenges.

"You tell me," I counter. Our hand cut fries were undoubtedly the best thing on our menu. I laugh out loud as I watch him close his eyes and savour the fry. His face lights up as he opens his eyes and stares back at me.

"They're even better than I thought they would be." His voice almost breaks, but his gaze does not waver, and I feel naughty to hold it for so long.

"Can I get you anything else?"

"I'm good...... for now." He adds as I walk back to the computer.

Hailey is almost giggling as I join her. "Wow Steph, considering you have barely noticed Mr. Single, you sure seem to be flushed, or maybe it's just boiling in here?" She teases and I gently push her away. She grabs the cutlery she's been prepping and heads off to prepare more tables for this evening.

Get a grip, Steph. Being a tomboy growing up, I've never been phased by boys. I am not the coy, shy girl batting her eyelashes at men, weak in the knees. It's just not my style. After a few drinks, sure, I can be an easy target for a smooth one liner and some playful flirtation, but I have never behaved like a silly schoolgirl towards any man. I have no idea why this handsome stranger is affecting me this way.

Checking the time, I realize my shift ends in 15 minutes. I take a quick walk around, ensuring my tables are clean and everything's ready for me to leave. As I walk by Mousy Curls, he gives me a thumbs-up to let me know it's all good. I smile in acknowledgement.

I roll the last of the cutlery, which will be needed for this evening, and fold some extra napkins. Nothing worse than a hovering server with nothing to do. "How's your shift been?" Kara arrives behind me. She's a friendly, twenty something brunette. Tall, thin and beautiful, she wouldn't look out of place in a modeling agency.

"It's been a bit quiet, but that means everything is ready for this evening." I smile.

"You are honestly the best, Steph. I love working after you, everything is so organised and prepared." Oh, I forgot, as well as looking beautiful, Kara is also the kindest girl you could ever meet. "So just table 8 left then? I can go and introduce myself if you wanna clock out a few minutes early." She offers kindly.

I hesitate. Although I would love to get off early, it might seem unprofessional. I don't want Kara to think I don't trust her though either. "Shall I just check if he needs anything before I go and then hand him over to you, is that good?" I ask easily. She nods in agreement, but she's already focused on next week's schedule and noting down her shifts.

"Is there anything else I can get you before I go?" His plate is bare, except for a little lettuce and half a slice of tomato.

He shakes his head, "leaving so soon? We were just getting to know each other." He sounds genuinely disappointed.

"Ha ha, I've got little people waiting on me." I explain.

He nods his understanding. "I'm sure your husband likes to have you at home in the evening too, I'm guessing." Aha, so I'm not completely misreading the signs.

"Well, as he's currently living in his mom's basement with his new girlfriend, I don't think it matters to him where I am." I can't believe I've just said that. I can see his face looks shocked. "I'm sorry, I have no idea why I just said that."

"No," he shakes his head. "You're fine." He reassures me. "It sounds like you dodged a bullet." The glint in his eyes returns as he smiles at me. "Actually, Steph, I've got an appointment. So, I think I'll just take the bill before you leave if that's ok?"

"Sure, I'll just get it for you." He probably wants to get out of here as fast as possible now he sees how lame I am. I print out his bill and arrive back at the table with the card reader. "Will you need this?" I ask casually.

He waves the reader away, "Nope, I've got cash, thanks. It was a pleasure to meet you, Steph. I hope to run into you again."

He gives me his large open smile, and again I try to put my finger on what seems so familiar to me about him. I know he's probably just a charmer, but something about him makes me want to sit here and listen to him all day. For the first time in years, I feel excitement and arousal stirring.

"Yes, you too." I smile back. "Have a great evening." I make my way back to the computer waiting politely for him to vacate his table. As he reaches for his coat, I notice the ripple of muscle in his forearm beneath the cotton of his shirt, and daydream that I could reach out and touch it. He chooses that moment to look my way, and gives me a little wave. I hope he doesn't spot me salivating over his muscles. I try to give a 'Oh I barely noticed you' expression and small wave in return. As he walks out the front door, I actually feel my stomach drop.

Pathetic! That's what I am. I'm a Mom. Technically, I'm still someone else's wife. What I'm certainly not is some smitten little schoolgirl. I need to get my shit together! Grabbing a tray, I set off to clear off his table. I wipe it down clean, drop the dishes off in the kitchen, and take the billfold to the till to close out his table before I leave.

I notice the $50 bill at once, and wonder if he left such a huge tip because he felt bad for me being a deserted single mom. Sound desperate much Steph, I scorn myself. As I place the bill into the drawer, I fold it and notice a handwritten note on the backside. **Steph, I never do this sort of thing and I know you're at work and need to be friendly to everyone, but I felt a real connection to you the moment I set on eyes on you. If there's any way you felt it too and weren't just being polite, please text me your number so I could ask you out? Shaun x** I could barely contain my excitement. He felt it too, I wasn't crazy. There had definitely been something. I quickly print off a duplicate of his bill and put it in the drawer, stuffing the original safely in my pocket. Today was a good day.

ϛ∂∾ℓ

"Steph? What's going on? I don't think you're even listening to any of us tonight." Monique nudges me from my reverie.

"Just lost in the moment." I smile. We're in the wings of the theatre. The kids need to line up, quietly, in their respective places for the next number. Luckily for new Mom's like me, most of these kids know exactly where they should be and when they should be there. So apart from idle chat with the other Mom's, we just help the kids with their costumes and are on hand if they need anything. Poor Charlotte has been posted on the other side of the stage and is stuck with both Sandra and Linda. I walked over there earlier, but it was akin to a military operation, so with a lot of eye rolling and giggling at Char, I made myself scarce.

"Hmmm, not lost in these moments, if you ask me." Gabrielle joins Monique who is intently staring at me.

I'm not going to get rid of them. "Ok, ok. I met the guy." I whisper.

"You met a guy, what guy." Wow Catherine really has good hearing, cause 2 seconds ago she was 5 feet away fixing some child's cape and I had no idea she was also part of this interrogation.

"No, she didn't say a guy, she said the guy. The guy who did what?" Sometimes the way Gabrielle words her sentences was enough to make you smile.

"Yep, not a guy. The guy. The guy I've deserved since day 1. The guy, God is sending me to make up for all Nate's awfulness. The guy who makes me feel like a schoolgirl again. That's the guy!" I tell the three of them who are hanging on my every word.

"Wow, it's very dramatic over here," Char joins, "so who's this guy then?" I fill the girls in on my kismet meeting.

"Stephanie, this is so romantic! You will have an amazing love story with this man, just like me and Marc. I am sure of it!" Monique hugs me in her excitement.

Gabrielle is jumping up and down. "I am so excited for you. A handsome stranger has come to be your prince. Have you texted him yet? Where are you going? Tell me everything." She's pulling at my arm in her excitement.

"I haven't texted him…" I'm trying to find the right words to explain that I wanted to wait until this evening when I was completely free, when I hear both Char and Catherine, murmuring in agreement.

"You're right Steph, you can never be too careful giving your info to a complete Stanger." Catherine warns.

Char places her hand protectively on my arm. "You've been through enough trauma in the last few months, you're right not to text him Steph. I totally understand. You want to be cautious." Um, no Char, I don't think you do.

I hold up my hand to stop anyone else accidently putting their foot in it and I continue. "I was going to explain that I want to wait until I am completely free this evening, but I can see you think I've misunderstood the situation. I guess because I was so naïve where Nate was concerned you all think I'm incapable of knowing the difference between a nice man and some old perv?" My outburst is irrational. I know by the stricken looks on their faces that I've hurt Catherine and Char's feelings. I feel awful. With my head down, I make my way to the washroom where I find an empty stall and promptly burst out crying.

What in the world is wrong with me? I mean, Char may be a bit controlling and overprotective, but her heart is absolutely in the right place. I can't believe I insinuated that she was inferring I was a brainless idiot. Well, I certainly felt like one now. As for Catherine, thank goodness my divorce paperwork is complete as I'll never be able to look her in the eye again. Shame and confusion wash over me, and I look around for a window I might be able to climb out of.

I hold my breath as I hear the 'swoosh' of the heavy door opening. The tap runs and the intruder washes their hands. "Stephanie, I am just checking you are ok. If you want me to leave, I will leave, but I also want you to know I am right here if you want to talk or need a hug." Monique's sweet French lilt dances its way through the door and I unlock the flimsy bolt.

I peer out the door shyly and she opens her arms. "Monique, I'm so embarrassed, I don't know what came over me." I pull back from her hug, willing her to see how wretched I feel.

"Awh Chérie, no one doubts you. Catherine and Charlotte know you meant no harm, you just got carried away in your emotions."

"Yes, that's exactly what happened. Why did I do that? Why did I behave so rudely? So unreasonably?"

Monique is laughing now. "You have finally been bitten. The love bug has knocked you over and you have been hit hard by the looks of things." She explains.

"But I'm not some schoolgirl, what's wrong with me?" I am perplexed why Monique is finding such enjoyment in my discomfort.

"This feeling you have right now, Stephanie, hold on to it tight. In years to come, when this man makes you mad, you will need to remind yourself how he and only he, made you feel when you first met. This is what I do with Marc, if ever he makes me mad. I close my eyes and I remember that first time I saw him. My right leg shook a little, like jelly, and in that instant I knew I would marry that man and make a life with him." She smiled at me and I knew she understood.

"It's not like that for everyone though, ok? In French we call this '*un coup de foudre*,' which, literally, means a lightning strike. Like an uncontrollable feeling you must act upon. In English you would say, love at first sight, but you North Americans, you know, you're not really believers. Us Latin people, the French, even the Brazilians like Gabrielle, we know it's real. We believe, and now Stephanie, you too, will be a believer."

Perfectly poised Monique was telling me she felt it too, and she was describing it perfectly. It had been exactly like a bolt of lightning. I have felt electrically charged all day. I am relieved to hear I am not alone.

"Thank you, Monique. I know I've behaved terribly, but thank you for being a true friend."

She wets a paper towel and passes it to me to wipe my face. "Don't be silly, we are all here for you. The others are just more cautious. You know they are more powerful women, they don't know how to give into love. To give up control. They are not there yet, and before today, neither were you. Try to remember they just want the best for you, ok?" This is the true essence of Monique. She could see everyone's point and respect everyone's opinion. "Now, clean your face and let's get back out there before anyone else shows up, ok?"

I splash a little more water on my face, wipe it down and nod. Time to face the music. As we exit the bathroom, I spy Catherine against the far wall and I make my way towards her. "Steph, I'm so sorry, I was way out of line. Me and my big mouth. See, this is why I keep to myself. I'm a social mess."

A lone tear slides down Catherine's face and I feel even worse. I wipe it with my thumb. "No, Catherine, I'm sorry. I got caught up in a lot of emotions today and I was just overwhelmed with it all. Please accept my apology, I'm so embarrassed and ashamed. I mean, after everything you've done for me, I can't believe I was so rude to you and the others."

"I think we honestly meant well, but in the excitement of the moment, we sounded mean spirited, and I know Char feels just as bad as I do. Can we chalk it up to backstage drama and forget about it?" Always the negotiator, Catherine has found the perfect solution for us all to save face.

"Yes please," I agree "and maybe a hug too because I feel so bad." I push. As she reluctantly opens her arms, I know our friendship is sealed forever. I squeeze extra hard. Not knowing when I may ever get the chance to hug her again. Considering she dislikes hugs so much, it feels like home.

"Ok enough, go find Char, I'm sure she feels awful." Catherine peels me off her and I head to the other stage side to seek Char.

I almost trip over her as she huddles on the floor, tying one of the chimney sweeps boots. "Oh Char, I was looking for you."

The boy thanks her and scurries off. I hold my hand out to her and pull her up from her squat. "I am beyond sorry Steph. The truth is, I have been so proud of you. You have become so strong and independent. You are not the broken little bird that Monique and I found that day in her car, and I am not your Mama bird feeding you worms."

"That's good, I don't like worms." I joke, trying to lighten the mood.

Char playfully nudges me. "I have had to start a lot of work on myself recently and I projected my worries on you, Steph. For that, I am truly sorry. I overstepped and that is unacceptable." I was stunned to be honest.

"Controlling, organising, always right Char is admitting to not having all the answers. Today must really be the best day ever!" I tease her. "I really appreciate that Char, especially as we both know I acted terribly and let my emotions run away with me. I'm truly sorry." My arms hug her tight to let her know that was the end of it. Subject closed.

"Steph, please take me away from here. These super moms are savage to the kids, and bitches to me. I can't take it anymore." She whispers into my hair.

I pull back, stunned that Char would ask me to protect her, and all at once I understood. She only speaks up for the people she cares for and loves, but she struggles to do it for herself.

I march over to Sandra and inform her. "We need an extra person on stage right, so I'm going to take Char to help us."

She looks at her clipboard. "Well then, we will be one short here. Has Michelle authorized you to change the numbers like this?" Wow, Sandra is clearly a woman who has waited all year to volunteer backstage in a children's production where she can challenge other moms.

"No, Sandra, I didn't think to bother Michelle with such trivial details on such an important night. I mean 3 of us are new on the other side so I figure it will be okay with you and Linda being such professionals, but I understand if you can't handle it. Don't worry, I'll let Michelle know you can't cope without Char and we'll work out another solution." I smile back at her smugly.

She makes a fictitious note on her clipboard. "Hmmm, I guess if Linda and I pull together, we can probably manage." She tuts.

"Yep, that's what I thought." I pull my face into a grimace, turn on my heel, grab Char's hand and march out of there.

Char and I arrive stage right, giggling hysterically. Some of the kids are looking at us and rolling their eyes, which only makes us worse. We fill in the others on the stage left showdown, and dissolve into laughter as the children finish their closing number. We applaud and cheer them loudly, still giggling as they leave the stage.

We gather our things, delighted the dress rehearsal was so successful, and excited for opening night the following evening. I wave goodnight to everyone as Lucy, Liam and I make our way home.

The kids chatter excitedly in the back seat about the dress rehearsal. "Mom, I wish we lined up more on your side of the stage. Some of the moms on the other side are a little strict." Liam catches my eye in the rear-view mirror and rolls his eyes at me.

"I'm sure everyone is just doing their best to ensure a smooth running of the performance, honey." I don't think this at all, but I don't want my kids feeling even more uncomfortable than necessary. It chokes me to have to defend either Sandra or Linda, but I believe in a united front and supporting the entire backstage team, even if some of them don't deserve it in my opinion. "As long as you're doing what you're supposed to and you're placed where you should be, they'll have no reason to be strict with you, ok? Do your best and let's make Michelle proud of all our hard work, right guys?" I ask them cheerfully, taking the focus off the other moms and placing it back where it belongs, on the show.

I turn the radio up to lighten the mood and we aptly sing along to 'Jesus, take the wheel'. I'm filled with hope, and the lyrics of the song suit my mood perfectly. I had been lost, and these past couple of months had been hard, but I felt certain I had come out the other side a stronger and better person. A more confident mom for the kids, even.

I turn the car into the driveway as the song is ending, and the kids grab their bags and head inside. Just as I am about to turn the key off in the ignition, a man's voice interrupts me through the radio. '**There are times in life when we all need Jesus to step in and guide us. This song goes out to each and every listener who**

needs a little faith tonight.' That voice! It's the same guy from the parking lot night with Char and Monique. How weird! I thought my radio was set to the usual 105.9 Country FM. Somehow, I am back on Christian radio again! As the announcer continues in his soothing melodic tones, I recognise the voice more and more, not just from the radio. Where else had I heard this voice? **'And that's all from me tonight, I hope you all tune in again tomorrow night for evening thoughts with Shaun.'**

It can't be... I turn the car off and hastily run into the house. In the kitchen, I open my laptop and google 'radio show evening thoughts with Shaun.' Within seconds, I find his photo on the Inspire Fm website. Even from the web, his caramel swirl eyes lure me in. It's him! When I had told the girls earlier that God had sent him to me, I was being a little flippant, but here he was! Literally a sign from God.

I grab his number from my bag and type out a text before I lose my nerve. **Hi Shaun, it's Steph from Doyle's. I just wanted to send you my number in case you wanted to connect.** I read it back and despite thinking it sounds lame, I hit send. Don't overthink this, Steph. Immediately, I see the three little dots appear and my hands shake in anticipation. He's writing back, omg, yes! The dots disappear and my heart sinks. A few seconds later they reappear. Maybe he regrets his note and is trying to find a way to tell me he's changed his mind?

Steph, today has been one of the longest of my life. Waiting all day, hoping to hear from you. I have been trying to find an acceptable excuse to show up at Doyle's again tomorrow. I'm sorry if this sounds lame, but I feel like it was destiny that I met you today.

I'm jumping up and down in the kitchen, whooping and smiling. Lucy comes in to get a drink for bed and eyes me quizzically. "Are you dancing mommy?" Her little brows furrow together as she tilts her sideways, looking at me expectantly.

"Just burning off some energy, Luce. You know, I had a great day and just want to dance it out." I smile at her. She grabs my hand and swirls underneath my arm. "Come on, let's get you ready for bed. I think I'll have an early night too."

I shoo her upstairs and grab my phone. **I'm gonna get my kids into their beds and then I'll text you as soon as I'm in mine.** I add a *winky* face emoji and hit send. Before I even reach the stairs, my phone pings back with a heart emoji. I bound up the stairs with more energy and excitement than I've felt in years.

Monique

Show Night

Marc and I arrive at the theatre 20 minutes before curtain call. We dropped Olivier off earlier for the pre-performance rehearsal and went to eat a quick bite at Bernard's Bistro. We make our way to the bar and I'm relieved to see Charlotte and Adam are already installed at a table towards the rear of the room. I wave and join the line at the bar with Marc to order a drink.

"What would you like Cherie?" Marc pulls out his wallet as we're next in line.

"I'll have a white wine, and can you get me a bottle of pop for during the performance, please?" I rub his shoulder appreciatively.

He nods, "go join your friend and Juju and I will bring the drinks over." I kiss him on the cheek. He really treats me like a princess.

I arrive at their table and lean forward to greet Charlotte with a kiss. "How are you two lovebirds doing?" I ask with a wink towards Adam.

"We're very excited for the show, aren't we Char." Adam seems to be teasing her.

Charlotte is shaking her head half laughing. "Honestly Monique, you change your outfit four times and your husband deems you a nervous wreck. I just want to look my best for my kids' debut performances." She explains, and I join in Adam's laughter. Poor Charlotte takes herself too seriously. Although in recent weeks, she's been like a different person. Open and questioning, eager to learn and discover new things. I smile at her, sipping her orange juice, proud of my friend and the steps she's taking to improve her mental health.

"Bonsoir everyone." Marc and Juliette arrive with our drinks and shake hands with Adam as Charlotte introduces them.

"What seats do you guys have? Marc and I are up in the balcony, it's our favourite place to sit. You can see the entire stage and it seems like the music dances off the ceiling up there." I smile at them.

"I took your advice and also got seats up there. We're in C11 and C12. I think we'll have a good view from there." Charlotte informs us.

"Perfect we're just the row in front of you. We'll all be together." I clap my hands together excitedly. "Hey, there's Gabrielle in line at the bar too." We look over and wave at her and a suave-looking gentleman with salt and pepper gelled back hair, who I presume is her husband Max.

The speaker system announces 5 minutes to curtain. We grab our drinks and head upstairs to find our seats.

I wave at Catherine and Stanton who are seated on the opposite end of our row and look around for Stephanie but can't seem to spot her. The theatre lights flicker as a two-minute warning for audience members to find their seats.

Marc takes my hand in his and smiles at me, I lean forward and kiss him. Since the announcement of the salon, were like a couple of honey-mooners all over again. The excitement of our hopes and dreams spilling over into our relationship. Juliette rolls her eyes at us dramatically.

As the lights dim into darkness, a hush falls over the 800 audience members and the curtains separate. The opening bars of *It's a hard knock life*, resonate from the orchestra and twelve younger girls in tattered pajamas delight us, dancing and singing across the stage. Stephanie's Lucy is one of the smallest in this cast and the uncertainty across her face is perfect for her orphan character. Catherine's Lexi has one verse as a solo, and she really is mesmerizing. Without even trying, she commands presence on the stage and her 1000-watt smile shines all the way up to us in the balcony. There is much whooping and hollering at the end of their number.

The next number features the entire cast. It's *the circle of life,* and all the harmonies and voices bring tears to my eyes. I glance back at Charlotte who smiles at me with her own glassy eyes. Even though you hear the kids singing at rehearsal, they're often split into groups and different rooms. It's really only now, you get to see how it all comes together. They're fantastic. This misfit group of kids, different ages, cultures all coming together and sounding as one.

The senior girls are up next with *Sandra Dee*. They're all over made up to the point of caricature and between jumping on the bed and rolling on the floor. Karla's wig falls off to riotous laughter from the audience. I'm not exactly sure if it's scripted, but it's hilarious and tears of joy stream down my face. I steal a sideways glance at Marc who is also laughing uncontrollably and I'm delighted he's enjoying the show as much as I am.

Linda's daughter Reese is next with a solo of *Somewhere over the rainbow*. Although it's sung technically perfect, it's hard to look past her stiff mean girl face. Poor thing, she'll have difficult years ahead of her as someone with great talent but a terrible attitude. Linda has really done her no favours bringing her up to be such an entitled brat. At the end of the number, the audience claps appreciatively and I spy Linda jump up from her seat in the middle of the theatre, jumping and clapping. I feel sad for her. As much as we're all proud of our kids and excited for them to do well, I would never want to be *that* Mom. Marc nods his head towards her and raises his eyebrow quizzically. "That's Linda." I whisper to him.

"Oh yes, of course it is.". He's heard stories about her over the years, he knows all about her. I squeeze his hand extra hard, thankful for the life we have built together.

Another few numbers and curtains fall for intermission. We make our way to the balcony bar and join Charlotte, Adam, Catherine and Stanton. Catherine introduces us all to Stanton and the three men join the line for the bar while us three girls search for a table. "Has anyone heard from Stephanie." I ask them.

"No, but I texted her and Gabrielle to let them know we would be at the balcony bar for intermission." Charlotte informs us. Of course, she did. Still organising everyone and everything, some things were unlikely to change. "So how are you finding the show Charlotte?" I remember Olivier in his first year and being blown away by the talent from all the kids.

"It's amazing, I've cried at every number, I don't know what's wrong with me. I must say Catherine, Lexi was superb in her number." I nod my agreement and Catherine smiles back at us proudly.

"I knew I would find you ladies at the bar." Laughs Stephanie as she approaches with a curly haired man in jeans and sports jacket. "I want you all to meet, Shaun. Shaun this is, Catherine, Monique and Char." He shakes hands with each of us and I subtly wink at Stephanie, letting her know this handsome man has my seal of approval. Actually, any man accompanying a single mom to her kids' theatre performance on their first date has my approval. Clearly this man is comfortable in his own skin.

Our husbands return from the bar, and further introductions are made just as Gabrielle and Max join us. "Isn't the show amazing?" Gabrielle enthuses to the group. "Lucy and Lexi were fantastic in their numbers." she declares.

"Not quite as entertaining as your Karla though." Catherine's eyes dance with amusement as she teases Gabrielle. "I still can't figure out if it was planned or not." She wonders.

"I don't think it was planned." Gabrielle's cheeks flush, "I'm sure Karla will be mortified, but it was funny." She giggles and the rest of us join her. The lights flash and dim. Stephanie, Gabrielle and their gentlemen, take leave making their way back downstairs.

As we settle back into our designated seats, I leaf through the program. Many local businesses advertise in it and I smile thinking how this time next year, we will take out a full-page advertisement for Elle. "What are you smiling at?" Marc leans over and whispers.

"Just thinking how next year we can also advertise in the program." I lift my face to kiss him and he squeezes my knee.

The opening number for the second act is from *Matilda*. Kids are dancing and running around the stage, and the entire number is perfect chaos. Children falling over other children and skipping over one another, all choreographed and timed to the second. I don't recall ever seeing any of this in practices and wonder how Mme Michelle brings it all together. She really is an amazing producer and director.

The youngest kids in the troupe sing a very heart pulling rendition of *Rainbow Connection*. There is a littler girl on the outside of the group who is distracted by an audience member in the front row. She keeps waving at them and pulling faces, and it only further adds to the innocence and delight of the performance. The audience cheer and clap. The little girl sticks out her tongue and wrinkles her nose at the instigator. I have no idea who the child is, but she is putting on a great side show to the amusement of every onlooker.

During the next few slow numbers, I start to feel sad. Sad that it's all coming to an end. This has been Olivier's 6th year in theatre and I worry that soon he will think he's too cool or get teased by the other sportier, tough boys at school and want to give up performing. In all the years of volunteering and helping, I have never encountered such great friends either. I feel deflated at the thought of not seeing them twice a week anymore. Maybe there's something Olivier and Levi could join? They seem to get along really well. I must mention it to Charlotte.

The curtains close for a brief moment, and we sit in the dark silence. They open and one by one a spotlight hits each chimney sweep on the rooftops. This is the number where Olivier has his solo part, and instinctively, I hold my breath until he's finished every note to perfection. Liam and Levi also sing and dance throughout this number, and I can see why Michelle chose it as the closing number. The crowd is clapping along as the younger children dance down the aisles to join the chimney sweeps on stage. The number finishes with endless calls of encores and much hooting and hollering. Marc squeezes my hand hard, pride beaming across his face as he stands and cheers for our boy. The curtain re-opens and the whole cast is onstage clapping and bowing. The audience is on their feet. A standing ovation is the least these kids deserve after all their hard work.

Our spirits are high. Downstairs we await the kids in the lobby. My patience has left me and I excuse myself from Marc and the others and sneak _{backstage} to find Olivier. As I open the backstage door, the hallway lights the side stage hallway. At once, Sandra marches over to me. "Do you need something, Monique?" She looks me up and down whilst tapping on her clipboard.

"No thanks, Sandra, just checking in on Olivier." I walk ahead.

"Michelle really prefers if audience members stay out in the foyer and not disturb us here backstage." She announces haughtily.

"Well, like you Sandra, I've been volunteering backstage for years and I am well aware of the protocols, thank you very much." I roll my eyes at her, thankful that at least with the end of the show I will have some respite from her death stares and judgemental tones. They say that kids can be mean, but honestly, they learn it from their mothers. I don't know if I ever met a bigger bitch than Sandra, and I would not tolerate another second of her. I hear her tutting and sniffing as I walk away and I smile to myself, glad to have ruffled her feathers.

I pass Mme Michelle in the stairwell. "Your best show yet Michelle, I honestly don't know how you continue to outdo yourself year after year." I congratulate her.

224

"Ha ha ha I don't do it alone, as you well know Monique. Without all your kids and the backstage Mom's help, there wouldn't be a show." She hugs me and I thank her for the amazing opportunities she's provided Olivier. "They only get what they earn Monique, Olivier works hard." I'm glad to hear such praise and wave her goodnight. I head downstairs towards the older boys' dressing room.

Levi is coming out as I approach. "Amazing job Levi, well done." I congratulate him. He blushes at my compliment. "Please, would you call into Olivier that I'm here?" I ask him before he leaves. He nods and re-enters the room.

"He'll be out in a minute." Levi re-appears. "Good night Monique" he calls and leaves in search of Grace to join Charlotte and Adam.

A few moments later Olivier appears. His hair is dishevelled from his hat in the chimney sweep number and his cheeks are pink with excitement. He loves to sing and dance. I am sure it was euphoric for him to have such a big part in the closing number. I hug him as hard as I can and he laughs.

"Whao... Maman, take it easy, there's a lot of people still around." He whispers and I follow his gaze towards the senior girls' dressing room door where Adriana has just appeared. She smiles in our direction as her cheeks fill pink with colour.

I look at Olivier enquiringly. "Something you want to fill me in on Olivier?" I tease.

He releases me from his embrace and with a smile that reaches all the way to the small creases in his eyes he says, "Not yet, but I will keep you posted." He sarcastically replies and urges me forward with his hand on my shoulder. We join the others in the lobby and Marc shakes his hand before enveloping him into a huge bear hug. Olivier is clearly embarrassed but also delighted at how proud we all are of him.

Charlotte and Adam wave goodbye as they leave with Levi and Grace. I catch Gabrielle's wink as they pass us, and I am delighted she is also aware of our young blossoming teen romance. I spot Stephanie hugging and congratulating Liam and Lucy and watch as Shaun high fives each child after he's presented them with a candy bouquet. The children squeal delightedly and I am reassured that Stephanie had fallen on her feet. Shaun seems to be the real deal.

I grab Marc's arm and we make our way through the thinning crowd. As we arrive outside, there's a small commotion in the corner. "I'm fine, honestly. Please, let's just go home." I hear the voice and at once recognize Catherine's no-nonsense tone.

I release Marc's arm and push my way through to the front where I peer at Catherine sitting on the concrete sidewalk, against the theatre's brick wall. I kneel beside her and take her cold hand

226

in mine. "Catherine, what is going on? Have you had a fall?" I look at her sensible shoes and wonder how she could have tripped.

"She didn't fall." Stanton fills me in. "She fainted. I want her to take 5 minutes before we set off, and she's arguing with me." Stanton is clearly laying down the law and I don't blame him.

I peer closer and although her face looks peaky; she seems fine. The scowl of disagreement tells me she wants to avoid further embarrassment and get out of there ASAP. "Did you eat today? Maybe it's low blood sugar? Are you diabetic.?" The thought just occurs to me.

"No, I am bloody not diabetic. It was just a bit warm in the theatre and as the cool air hit me, I came over all funny but I'm fine now. Please tell Stanton I'm fine. I want to go home. Look at poor Lexi, this is her evening. I look over at Lexi who is in no way concerned with her Mom sitting on the floor. She dances on the sidelines, entertaining the exiting crowds oblivious to her mom's distress. Many people congratulate her as they pass, and her smile beams back at them.

"I don't think you're stealing any of Lexi's limelight, don't you worry about that." I reassure Catherine and despite the situation we start laughing "Stanton, I think she's ok, can Marc and I help you bring her to the car?" Marc has joined us and is standing just behind Stanton.

"Actually, would you mind waiting here with her and I'll run and bring the car up front." He offers. We nod in agreement and Catherine rolls her eyes. She can see it's futile to argue and leans her head against the bricks as we wait for Stanton to reappear. Luckily Lexi is not one to let an audience go to waste, and she continues to entertain us until I see the white Lincoln roll up in front of the theatre.

Marc and I assist Catherine up, and we walk slowly towards the car. "Do you have any pain anywhere?" I ask her as she bends into the car.

"Just the never-ending embarrassment of being sat on the floor outside." She admits.

"Hey, don't worry about that, I'll tell people you had too much to drink. How's that?" I mock her.

"Oh, that would be perfect Monique, thanks so much." The words drip from her lips sarcastically and we wave them off, with little Lexi hanging her head out the back window still singing.

Marc, Olivier, Juliette and I cross the street towards our own vehicle, humming the chimney sweep song and I offer a silent prayer to God that all will be well with Catherine.

Charlotte

Cast Party

The kids' cast party is being held at a local banquet hall. There's food, games and dancing. Rehearsals and performance nights are a lot of hard work, and the party allows everyone to blow off a little steam and have some fun.

Monique advised us that most of the Mom's stay at the party and grab a table near the bar and have a few drinks. It seemed the perfect solution to end our theatre experience, and I was happy to have this final outing with us all here. Without doubt we would remain friends and still get together, but I feared we may not all end up in the same groups again by chance like this. It really was serendipity to meet these amazing women. I had no idea; I needed them. It's almost crazy how individually we have nothing in common, but together we have everything.

I enter the hall and find Monique who has already secured us a coveted booth. "Thank goodness you're here." She murmurs to me as I hug her. "Twice Linda's come over to see if she can help me with anything. I would never want to be rude but get the message lady, we're exclusive not inclusive." She exaggerates and I slide onto the bench, giggling.

"Ohh what are these?" I gesture towards the white boxes tied with ribbon set out at each place setting.

"Just a little something I got for each of us. I wasn't going to display on the table like this, but I had to discourage Linda from inviting herself to sit down." She explains.

"That is so thoughtful, Monique." I'm excited to see what the boxes hold. A sneaky part of me hopes they're facial products to promote the new salon. "How is it going with plans for Elle?" I'm eager to hear all about it.

"It's a little overwhelming, but we've had a designer in who has made some 3d drawings to show us how we can make more of the space and I think together, Marc and I are coming up with some superb ideas. Maybe too many ideas." Her forehead crinkles in mock worry. "It will be a lot of hard work. but I can tell it's going to be worth every second. What about you, Charlotte?

How have things really been?" Her hands grab mine and she looks at me concerningly.

"Actually Monique, I'm proud to admit, I'm doing better than ever. My pills have been life changing, but working with my therapist and concentrating on my own mental health has helped tremendously. Sometimes by early evening I get that twisty tight feeling of anxiety across my chest and wonder what it is and I realize, I'm late taking my pills. I forget I lived with that anxious feeling all day, every day. I look back and wonder how I even made it through. If it wasn't for Adam, God only knows what I would have become." I smile at her. I'm no longer embarrassed to admit I was drowning. I simply feel blessed to have made it out the other side. "It probably sounds ridiculous, but I'm writing a self-help book for other women like me. For the mis-understood 'Karens' in this world, who think that controlling and organizing other people is their job. I honestly thought I was doing my best and my views were the only way to grow and move forward and now I no longer believe any of it. I've become a hypocrite. The ideas I once held as 'the only way' or 'truth' are just one of several options now. I no longer see right and wrong, just choices with different consequences." I realize I'm rambling and probably boring poor Monique.

She grabs my hands and squeezes them tight. "This is *fantastique* Charlotte. Too many books are written by perfect people. This is not what we need. We need more imperfect people to admit we don't have all the answers and to teach us to open our minds. I will be the first person to buy your book and I will place it proudly on the shelf of the salon for our clientele to enjoy." Monique doesn't do things in half measures, and my heart fills with gratitude for this amazing friend.

"Quite the heart to heart going on here ladies, eh?" Steph ribs us as she slides along the opposite bench. She is positively glowing. Her eyes seem to dance merrily as she sits there positively beaming at us.

"Wow Stephanie, you're glowing! Is Shaun working some kind of magic on you? Have you been sexting with him already?"

"Monique, you can't say that." For once, even I am shocked by Monique's brazenness.

"If it, was you or me, Stephanie would say much ruder, cruder things to us." She defends.

Steph burst out laughing, nodding her head, and I reluctantly agree. "Yeah, she's right Steph, you would." I join in.

"Laugh all you like; nothing can bother me." She says just as both Gabrielle and Catherine arrive.

"Shall I give you ladies a minute to get settled in?" A red-haired server with thick kohl eyeliner and crimson lips stands at the head of our booth.

"Oh, I'm more than ready." Monique declares, and the rest of us agree. "I'll have a cosmopolitan please." She orders.

"That sounds good, I'll have one of those too please." Agrees Steph.

Gabrielle shouts down, "me three."

Catherine looks over to me to order next. "I'll have a white wine spritzer please, heavy on the spritzer please." I smile.

The red head turns to Catherine. "I'll have just the spritzer please with a dash of lime." I wonder if Catherine wanted to order a non-alcoholic drink to make me feel less alone from the others.

"I can have the odd drink and it doesn't affect my meds," I say to no one in particular. "It's just if I have three or four, I'll be in bed all day tomorrow sedated from my meds, but I'm ok to have one or two." I feel I owe them an explanation after all the support and love they've shown me.

They all smile at me and reassure me, I'm doing great. When I look at Catherine, she can't quite meet my eye and I hope I haven't embarrassed her.

"How are you feeling, Catherine?" Monique interrupts. The rest of us look from Monique to Catherine confused.

"Did we miss something?" Asks Steph.

"Catherine was feeling unwell after the performance night last week and had a little fainting episode." Monique elaborates. "Was it just low blood sugar after-all?" She looks at Catherine.

Catherine's face turns beet red, and it's clear she wishes Monique had not divulged this information with the rest of us.

"You look great now anyways." I try to change the subject. "Probably just something you ate, right? Speaking of food, I am starving. Gabrielle, can you pass me down a menu, please?" Gabrielle passes menus to each of us and I catch Monique mouthing a thanks to me. We all spend a minute or two looking at the menus and discussing different options when Catherine clears her throat.

"I'm sorry, I know I've made you all feel awkward. It's just I am still struggling with being open and sharing private stuff, but I'm working on it, I promise." She smiles at us.

Steph throws her arm around her and we all laugh as Catherine physically winces at being touched. "Listen, once two women insist on climbing into your car, while you're wailing, having a breakdown, there're no boundaries to be set after that. Monique and Char are full-on, and now even I've become like them." She laughs, "there's no escaping it." Steph jostles Catherine a final time before removing her arm from around her shoulders.

The server arrives with our drinks and we put in our food order. The tables around the bar have filled and we decide it's best to get our requests in early.

"It's early on and I really shouldn't say anything yet, but I'm pregnant." Catherine whispers across the table as the server leaves.

"Are you serious? Oh my God, I'm so excited." Steph flings both her arms around Catherine and holds on tight. The rest of us look at each other in awe.

"Congratulations Catherine, what a blessing." I reach across the table and grab her hand as Steph reluctantly releases her. Monique and Gabrielle also congratulate her, and we inundate Catherine with our endless questions.

"Thank you, girls. Stanton and I are very excited, but we haven't even told Lexi yet. Considering my history, nothing is a sure thing but we are hopeful, so I'm gonna ask everyone to put a pin in their questions for another month or two, is that ok?" She asks quietly?"

"Yes, of course it is Catherine, and thank you so much for trusting us with this information." I tell her, "now who's next in the hotspot?" I look around and we all laugh.

"Good evening ladies, I hope you're all enjoying yourselves." Michelle has come over to give our table a visit. "You five really seem to have bonded this season."

"You're always welcome to join us." I slide down the bench to make a space for her.

She shakes her head. "Thanks so much, but I've already got a seat with some of the other moms over there." I'm surprised when I see a very subtle eye roll and let out a small giggle. Michelle winks at us, "I hope to see you all back again next year." She bids us a good evening amidst us all calling out our thanks and appreciation.

"So do we get to open our little gifts yet?" Steph is as excited as a child waiting for a party bag at a birthday.

"Sure," Monique agrees, "they're nothing big, just something I saw and thought was made for us." She explains.

I untie the curled ribbon and open the box. Inside is a cocktail glass with the words 'Unicorn Mom' in fuchsia pink. "These are amazing Monique," Gabrielle enthuses. "Thank you so much, I love it." She immediately pours her Cosmo into her new glass and we all follow suit.

"Cheers, to us, The Unicorn Mom's." Monique reaches her glass into the centre of the table and we all lean forward to clink glasses together.

"It's official, we're a club now." Steph smiles.

"Am I the only one who doesn't know the meaning of a 'Unicorn Mom'?" Catherine asks warily.

We all turn toward her dumbfounded. She is always dressed in current style and a little younger than Monique and I. I was surprised she had never heard the term. "It's a way to define, the imperfect mom." Monique explains.

"Yeah, it's a mom who enjoys drinking and has a great sense of humour." Steph expands.

"Basically, it's us." I declare, and we all clink glasses once again, delighted with ourselves.

∾∾

After we've eaten and tasted everything on each other's plates, Catherine apologizes. She needs to get going. We all remember how tiring the early stages of pregnancy and bid her goodnight as she sets off to find Lexi.

Steph also takes this as her excuse to leave, and we all wink and make jokes how she must get home and say her prayers. "Geesh guys, Shaun maybe a host on Christian Radio but I think he's gonna be a devil in the bedroom." She guffaws and we all wave goodnight to her.

"So, Monique, I think you might see a little more of my Adriana in the non-too distant future. She and Olivier are non-stop texting." Gabrielle informs Monique and I.

"I thought there was something. He denied it when questioned, but I didn't really believe him." Monique laughs easily. "Actually Gabrielle, I was hoping you and I might get to see a little more of each other too." She states.

A look of confusion crosses Gabrielle's face as I also wonder what Monique means.

"Marc and I had a designer into the salon yesterday and she suggested the upstairs rooms would make a great yoga studio and personal trainer instruction room and I thought you might be just the woman for the job."

Gabrielle's beautiful chestnut eyes instantly fill and shine in the over head glaring light. "Monique, are you serious, are you offering me a job?" She can't believe her luck and I am delighted for her. I had reservations when I introduced these two, but they compliment each other perfectly.

"More than a job, really. I mean you'll have to come and visit the space and we'll have to sit down and talk with Marc, but I was hoping we could work out some kind of partnership for the upstairs. What do you think?"

"I think this sounds amazing. I've spent the last few weeks looking for rental spaces and not been able to find anything that would make sense financially. This is literally my dream come true, Monique." Gabrielle reaches across the table and grabs her hand. "Thank-you Monique, thank you for thinking of me."

"We'll have to iron out the fine details, I'll text you tomorrow to come and see the studio, ok?" Monique offers and Gabrielle readily agrees.

Our three phones ping simultaneously. A notification that our group chat has been changed to 'Unicorn Mom's.' A moment later a picture of Steph comes through, drinking from her unicorn cup. **'Cheers Biches'** her message reads. Our phones ping, ping, ping as we all respond.

The party is winding down and Levi, Olivier, Grace, Karla and Adriana come to find us in the bar.

"And this is my signal to go home," I announce as I smile knowingly at Levi. His cheeks look flush. Adriana stares at him adoringly. Poor thing, she looks as though she's fallen hard. I'll be having a word with Levi to make sure he treats her right. Grace and Karla are looking at their phones and giggling. They've all had a great night.

I stand up and slip my coat on. I look at these two formidable women and know there's nothing left to say. We have our whole lives left to continue to grow together, and I shall be grateful for every moment.

As I wave goodbye and head for the door with Levi and Grace, I turn on my heel. "G'night Biches." I yell. I catch Sandra rolling her eyes just as Monique and Gabrielle dissolve into laughter. My work here is done. For now, anyway!

The Unicorn Moms

Made in the USA
Monee, IL
07 May 2021